Twisted Hearts

August Knights MC

Book #2

The Twisted Series

By:

Keta Kendric

Keta Kendric/Hot Pen Publishing, LLC
P.O. Box 55060
Virginia Beach, VA 23471

Cover: Steamy Designs

Editing: Tammy Jernigan

ISBN: 978-1-956650-13-6/Twisted Hearts

Contents

Synopsis

Megan: How the hell did he do it? Aaron messed with my mind and twisted up my heart, but my body had never been so splendidly ravaged. Stepping away from the August Knights Motorcycle Club was easy, but leaving Aaron was killing me. Was it crazy of me to want to subject myself to the madness the group stood for because I couldn't shake Aaron's hold on me? I couldn't go back. I had to consider his safety. I couldn't allow my twisted past to go crashing into the turbulent life he led.

Aaron: How the hell did she do it? Megan had cracked my chest open and filled it with a riot of crippling emotions I couldn't shake. Letting Megan go wasn't easy. Was it crazy of me to go chasing her after we agreed that it was over? I had to find her. My infatuation with her didn't leave me any other options. In my quest to find Megan, I discovered that she had secrets, deep dark ones I could have figured out if I hadn't gotten distracted. I would make her tell me what she was hiding in that twisted mind of hers—*or else*.

Warning:
Please be advised. This book is a multicultural romance that contains explicit sexual content and is intended for adults. If you are easily triggered by morally grey characters, explicit language and graphic violence, this is not the book for you.

Chapter One

Aaron

I dealt mainly in the weapons portion of my motorcycle club's illicit business, but as a member of one of the most notorious MC's in Florida, one tended to get involved in and see the harsh reality of the drug side of the business too.

The addicts. I despised them. They were weak, pathetic fucks who let something like a piece of crack or meth control their lives and steal their minds. They stole from their family, killed, cheated, and sold their souls to the devil to chase the temporary glory the drug gave them.

I never understood an addict's mentality. Didn't understand how they let something so insignificant run their lives and lead them to make decisions they never would have otherwise. How could they do just about anything for another taste, another hit, another high? I didn't understand what they got out of it, other than a feeling they loved so much they were willing to do anything to experience it again.

Two weeks had passed since Megan disappeared, walked the fuck right out of my life without so much as uttering a goodbye. I hated her for what she did to me. I hated her for making me feel things for her, with her, and about her.

She had intoxicated my system and filled me with needs I never had before. She made me want her in ways I never even fantasized about. For fuck's sake, I had gotten a checkup so I could fuck her without a condom.

I damn sure didn't tell her that she was the only woman I ever fucked in my adult life without one. She would likely have assumed otherwise. However, when the need had risen inside me, so strongly to have her without anything between us, I needed to satisfy it. Just like I needed to find her now, to satisfy my need to see her, hold her, and fuck her brains out for leaving me.

I had to have her even when my father warned me not to touch her. She ignited my body, stimulated my mind, and delved into my spirit. If it were a sin to lust after someone as badly as I yearned for Megan, then I would shake the devil's hand right before walking my ass through his fiery gates.

The worst part was she made me understand how hardcore addicts suffered when they craved their drug of choice and couldn't get it. Megan had no idea she was a fucking drug to me, a fix I'd gotten used to taking whenever my need became too great.

Fuck, most times, I couldn't even wait until the need for her overcame me. She had me so wide open that I fucked her every moment I could. She was the kind of drug I didn't have to chase because she was so giving and willing and ready whenever I wanted a hit.

Now that I didn't have her, I couldn't think, or sleep or fucking eat a damn thing. Instead of having nightmares about all the poor fuckers I've killed in the past, sweat-drenching dreams about the many ways I had taken her all over my house haunted me. Dreams that left my dick hard enough to cut through metal. Dreams that had me calling out for her when I knew she wouldn't answer. Dreams that left me cold and empty, devoid of the sparks she ignited within me.

I often found myself staring into space when people talked to me, her image filling my head instead of me focusing on what was being said. Nausea overtook me on the third day without her, my body going through withdrawals like nothing I'd ever experienced.

Able now to sort through the haze she left me in and focus, a fucking big-ass red flag I neglected to notice, finally occurred to me. I had no idea who Megan was and where she had gone until she was gone. Her name, Megan Jones, was common, so there was no way I could weed her out of hundreds of thousands of others with the same name.

When I really put effort into my thinking, I realized she had never mentioned what state she was from. Megan had driven up over a month ago in a rental car according to my father, but when it was time for her to leave, she mentioned going to the airport.

I had been fucking the woman for weeks, shared my deepest secrets with her, and killed three men with her, but I didn't *really* know her. For fuck's sake, she helped me bury the bodies, had cleaned the crime scene in my kitchen, and I never bothered to ask her where she was from.

Most women would have been offended, hurt or angry, but not Megan. No, she was different.

She mentioned having a hard life growing up in foster care, but she never bothered to disclose the details on how she became so hardened. A soft innocence added a depth to her outside appearance and made her beautiful to the eyes, but she harbored the same kind of darkness I carried around inside me. There was a seething angry darkness flowing through her that allowed her to endure horrific scenes and violent situations that would have had hardened criminals cowering in a corner.

Megan was like me, twisted up in the head enough that she could look a man in the eye and pull the fucking trigger. She inserted herself into our MC, agreed to work for us to pay off a debt she *claimed* her sister owed us for drugs. Who in their right mind would do something so insane? I'd asked her that question many times and never got a straight answer from her.

A few days after Megan left me, I started questioning my MC about her, gathering any information she might have shared with them. All I found was more questions. No one, including my father, the president of our MC, knew Megan's true identity.

My cousin, Jake, had informed me that he didn't remember her sister, the one she was *supposedly* working the debt off for. My father, Shark, claimed he had checked her background, and I believed him. Despite his backwoods ways, he would never have let Megan anywhere near our inner circle if the story she fed him hadn't checked out.

He insisted that he confirmed with a medical professional that her sister was in the Jefferson Rehabilitation Facility in Alabama, based on information Megan had provided to him. How he got a medical facility to divulge patient information was a trick I would have to learn from him one day.

Although I knew they weren't allowed to reveal patient information, I gave it a try anyway. They wouldn't tell me shit, even when I pretended to be a detective and fed them a fake badge number.

My father called the police station to confirm the two detectives Megan claimed she'd spoken to pending her visit with our MC. She said it was to make them aware of her decision to meet with the August Knights of her own free will.

In the thirty days Megan was a cleaning lady, cook, and bartender for us, she found ways to earn my MC's respect. First, she shot a man who would have killed my Uncle Wade. And a few weeks later, she killed a man inside my kitchen, one who'd come to take my life.

The most shocking revelation of it all was that she was the epitome of what my MC was supposed to hate. We were known for being a racist MC. Even though, in my opinion, most of our views and attitudes were strategic tactics to strike fear into the hearts of rival MC's, gangs, or anyone with the balls enough to test us. Granted, there were members who were racist assholes, but a good number of us lived with the perception because it provided an extra layer of danger to our 13eputetion.

The idea of a black woman getting into our inner circle deep enough for us to freely reveal our secrets to her was incredulous. A fucking miracle. It's just not supposed to happen. To have possibly fallen in love with her wasn't supposed to fucking happen either. My plan today to ditch work to go in search of her was damn sure not supposed to fucking happen.

***

With my phone glued to my ear, I heaved a heavy sigh and rolled my eyes every time I was transferred from one office to the next. One detective's desk to the other, I kept bouncing until I was transferred to someone who *might* be able to help me. I clamped my eyes shut and tuned out most of the detective's monotone statements. He didn't confirm the shit I was asking him about.

"Thank you. Appreciate the time," I said, ending the call, my enthusiasm as flat as the detective's tone.

It was the criminal task force unit in Crock County, Florida. The one Megan claimed she visited before engaging our MC. Neither of the numbers listed on the business cards she gave my father worked and the detectives named on the cards didn't work for that precinct.

As a matter of fact, no one at the precinct knew who the hell the detectives were and had never even heard of Megan Jones. Who the hell had my father talked to when he confirmed Megan's story.

I stared at my phone. Could Megan have masterminded her way into my MC?

A sick feeling in my gut was telling me that her story was all a front. Megan was not who she claimed to be.

Had she devised a plan that had allowed her to infiltrate the August Knights? If so, why?

Why would Megan do it? What possible reason could she have for wanting to get in bed with the likes of us? Did she even have a damn sister? It was funny that she hadn't mentioned her sister unless I asked about her. She'd not called to check on this infamous sister during her stay with me either.

Had Megan pulled off the ultimate scheme? Was she a deep cover agent, willing to do anything to catch her criminal or gather information? Was she working for a rival MC?

She couldn't have been a cop because she killed a man in cold blood right in front of me and hadn't shown a hint of remorse. She also shot a man in front of my father and dozens of MC members.

Was *Megan* even her name? Who was this woman and why was it beginning to feel like me and my MC had been manipulated? She got so close that the idea of what she knew about us scared me, and I didn't scare easily.

When I asked questions about Megan, it stirred suspicions with the rest of my MC. They too were now toying with the idea of how easily they allowed her to manipulate them.

I backed off when the whispers of suspicion began. I didn't need to get them excited. They would go off on a half-cocked witch hunt without knowing the full story.

However, I did feel the need to inform my father since he was the MC's president. All eyes were on me when I pulled up.

"Aaron," someone called out. I shot a head nod in the general direction of the voice, not giving a damn who it belonged to. Stepping inside the clubhouse was no better. They didn't have to be looking directly at me for me to sense them watching.

As soon as I glanced at my father across the room and kept walking to the back, he followed me. He stepped into the board room and pulled the door closed behind him. His cocked gaze remained pinned on me the whole time.

"We need to talk about Meagan."

His ears perked and he sat hard in his chair. It only took me a few minutes to offload my speculations, what I discovered, and that I believed Megan had tricked us.

"Kill her. Hunt her down. You need to kill her, " he said, his voice remained level while ordering me to kill a woman.

"Motherfucking, fuck."

I blew out a long breath while he proceeded to curse for what felt like a straight hour.

"That fucking bitch."

I didn't say a word while Megan became every combination of words that you could successfully use with the word *bitch*. He damned her to the far reaches of hell while I listened and watched, bored.

His ego was so high on the pedestal he propped it up on that having someone get one over on him had him blowing all his gaskets and loosening every screw pining his brain to his skull.

If there was one thing Shark couldn't stand, it was being made a fool of. Neither could I. I just handled it better.

Me? I was patient enough to figure out the truth. I would dig until I found answers or found Megan, whichever came first.

Now, I cursed myself for saying anything to my father before I found out the full story behind my speculations. It vexed the hell out of me that none of us knew who Megan truly was or where she came from other than what she'd divulged to us. It proved that I was just as possessed by the glamour she used on us as everyone else.

Shark pounded his fist into the table, making the solid wood vibrate. I left him to his tantrum and allowed my mind to drift.

Where the hell had she gone? We didn't even know where she came from. The only thing I believed at this point was that she truly was a writer. She had written a full manuscript when we were together, and the writing style matched that of her books I'd downloaded and read.

Therefore, I believed one way of tracking Megan down was by her books. I'd read three of them so far including the rough draft of the manuscript she wrote while with me.

In the books that I read, I noticed she left her social media contact information in the back for her readers to interact with her. Those contacts might be my only shot at tracking her down.

I stood, eyeing my father who wasn't cursing but still very, much hot.

"I have a few things to take care of. This stays between me and you."

He nodded, and the last thing I saw before I stepped away was his face drawn into a tight angry knot.

Chapter Two

Aaron

After my first few attempts at tracking Megan down failed, I realized that I would need help. The idea that she might have tricked me and my MC in some way for some reason, was starting to curb the sexual ache and need I had for her.

I even went as far as to send her several emails using the contact information in the back of her books, but she didn't take the bait. Instead, she thanked me for reading her books and offered to send me a free copy of any of her books I hadn't read yet.

My phone vibrated in my pocket, snatching me away from the ideas swirling in my head. It was my friend, D. Derrick Michaels was a computer geek I met and became friends with while in the military. He was no longer in the military, but he offered services that you couldn't readily get on the open market.

D offered the kind of tech services that could send a person to prison for a long time. He presented a quiet, nerdy persona, but I knew better. The man was in my military unit. I'd seen him kill with the same quiet ease in which he lived.

D's services were requested whenever I needed to track down someone. He was a major part of the reason I was able to track enemies for our MC or anyone who convinced themselves that they could hide from me.

Earlier today, I scanned D a copy of Megan's drivers' license. I had taken it from her purse as a security measure, a day after she entered my house. I also gave D her social media information and a listing of all the sites where her books were sold.

"D, what do you have for me?" I asked, forcing a smile over the deep frown on my face as I drove.

A long pause followed the question before D's calm voice flowed through the phone.

"Knox, I got nothing but questions man. Are you sure you want to pursue this woman?"

D called me by my last name, sticking to the way we were trained to address each other in the military.

For him to ask me that question, he must have stumbled upon something that concerned him.

"Yes, I'm sure," I finally answered him. "Why are you asking? What did you find?"

My foot eased off my accelerator a notch, preparing to listen to what D was about to say. I could hear him sigh on the other end of the line.

"That's just it. I didn't find a damn thing. This woman has hidden herself under so many layers that I can't find out who the hell she is, even with a popular writing career. Are you sure she's this writer Megan Jones or was that a cover?"

Confused, I shook my head although D couldn't see it. "Yes. She sat in my house and wrote a full manuscript fast as shit, and from what she let me read, the shit was legit. I was buying it and I don't even read that stuff." I didn't tell D I'd read four of her books, including an un-released manuscript and had ordered more. Her books gave subtle peeks into her mind, a mind I was sure held more secrets than a confessional.

"She writes under the pen name Megan Jones, but as far as her real name goes, I can't make a connection with a real live person. Hell, for all I've found, Megan Jones could be her real name," D informed me. The hint of con-cern in his voice wasn't lost on me.

"When I attempted to get into her finances to see where the money from her books sales was going, I dis-covered that the money goes through an organization called the Phoenix Foundation, which then distributes it to other non-profit organizations."

The crease in my forehead deepened. "What? Are you saying she doesn't use any of the money for herself? How the fuck is she living?" I asked D, aware he hadn't found the answer yet, or he would have told me.

His update had me reeling. Working off a debt for her sister was a fucking rouse if Megan had the ability to give money away. Why did she choose to spend thirty days among my MC?

D continued. "Man, that's one of the questions I've been trying to find answers to. When I hacked into her social media accounts, they were all under Megan Jones, but that was it; no state, city, or anything associated with an actual person. She gives the bare minimum as far as information goes and the details she gives leads to dead ends. All I know is she's someplace in the United States and I ain't even one hundred on that."

When D started using slang terms, I knew something had stumped him. I wasn't sure it was something about himself that he noticed. D was the whitest white boy I knew but had grown up in one of the worst areas in Philly, so he was about as hood as they came. Every now and again, you could hear it in the way he talked.

While there were men who ran around playing hard, D had shared stories of his childhood that rivaled my own. He also saw as much action on the streets of Philly as we saw as soldiers in the active war zones.

"Knox, I can't tell you yet who the hell this Megan is and where the hell she's at, but I'm still searching. The driver's license you scanned me is registered to a legit Texas address. But, Knox, get this shit. When I hacked into the DMV and found the Megan Jones that belonged at that Texas address, it was not the same Megan Jones whose face was on the license you scanned me. Your pretty brown Megan has put her face on a pretty *white* Megan's driver's license."

"What the fuck?" I asked, not believing what I was hearing. Who the fuck had I been sleeping with for two weeks? Who the fuck had I been obsessing over?

These updates had me beyond pissed and so irritated, the vein in my forehead throbbed. Megan had played me. She played my entire MC, pretending to be someone else so she could get whatever the hell she wanted from us. The worst part of the situation was, I still didn't know what the fuck she wanted from us or why.

"I'll keep digging." D's voice lured me away from the dark anger that nipped at my mind and planted deadly intent there. "I have another assignment. It's a field assignment, but I'll work on this for you when I can. I'll call you later to let you know what else I find out."

"Thanks, D," I managed before hanging up. I didn't bother D when he had what he called *field assignments*. There were times when he went black, and I knew it meant an illegal operation that involved violence and likely death.

My fingers clenched tighter around Megan's driver's license. My intentions were to have D check Megan out the day I took her license from her purse, but I got distracted. The sex, the cooking, and her ability to make me feel like I was something special. Even the way she handled the occasional bouts of violence that crept into my life had blinded me to who she was under the surface. Masterfully, she seduced me and made me see only what she wanted me to see.

The driver's license, the only thing I had of hers wasn't truly hers. Hot wasn't a strong enough word to describe me at this point. I wanted to hurt someone. All of that longing and need I'd had for Megan was being eaten away by pure unadulterated rage.

Through gritted teeth, I grumbled at the license in my hand. "When I find you, whoever the fuck you are, I'm going to make you sorry you ever met me."

Chapter Three

Megan

I couldn't stop licking my lips or stop my nails from clawing into Aaron's back. "So fucking good." I chanted dirty words at him, but he was a man who didn't need any encouragement.

The man could fuck so good that I was prepared to drop my panties anytime he wanted sex. It didn't matter if I was eating, sleeping or cleaning. I would stop whatever the hell I was doing and let him take me any way he wanted it.

"Shit, baby, you're fucking me so damn good. You're going to make me cum."

And that was exactly what I was about to do. Every time he sank into me, he brushed past my G-spot and reached as far as he could go inside my pussy, stroking an untapped desire; a mixture of pain and pleasure that drove me clean out of my fucking mind.

Jesus, his dick was so big and delicious. Aaron had the biggest dick I'd ever seen in person, and he knew how to use it masterfully.

I'd never experienced anything like it, and I couldn't get enough. Like now, one of my legs was wrapped around his back. The other was raised high in the air as his strong hand gripped and pushed against the back of my ankle.

He eased up on the forceful pounding and switched to the grinding thrust that left him planted deep inside me. God, he was massaging every pleasure zone, making me bend and fold and flex to his every move.

I couldn't breathe. I couldn't think. I couldn't do anything but scream for him to keep fucking me.

Finally, when I believed my heart was about to burst, an orgasm ripped through me with the force of a hurricane. Stars sparkled bright before they fell and rained down pleasure all over me.

My mattress danced under my startled body as I sprang up with a start. Harsh breaths got away from me as my hand bobbed up and down atop my heaving chest. I kicked angrily at my covers, knocking them away from my legs, upset that my pleasure wasn't real. The steady flow of cool air coming from the vent above my bed did nothing to cool my hot body.

It was another one of those pussy-wetting dreams about Aaron, the unforgettable man, and the two-week sex marathon we shared. I regret walking away from him, but I didn't have a choice. In the weeks I spent with him, we slept together so many times I lost count. Every time was pure magic.

The man had lured me into every position imaginable. Aaron had coaxed countless orgasms out of me. This man had encouraged me to embrace my sexual appetite, one I wasn't aware I possessed. With him, I had thrown my insecurities out the window and enjoyed our time together.

Aaron had gifted me the best sexual experiences in my life. Now, I crave him. My body ached for him. I longed to feel him possess me. I was convinced that no one would ever be able to do to me what Aaron had done. No one else would ever measure up. No other man would ever be able to fill me up to near bursting with not only pleasure but strong hard dick.

Somehow I managed to gather the strength and left Aaron, one of the sexiest and finest men to ever cross my path. He should put a patent on techniques for fucking because he turned me out the first time.

His tall, medium frame was built of pure sin and seduction. His tight abs, his sensuous lips, his dark blond hair, his piercing blue eyes, and his collection of tattoos was nothing short of a modern marvel. The man had enough in his sexual arsenal to stop any woman in her tracks.

Before meeting Aaron, I wasn't into sex other than to satisfy my urge when I got one. Before him, I could literally go months without so much as a twinge of desire awakening within me. Now, weeks without him had me twitchy like a fucking addict.

Frantic hands, contorted face, legs jumping, I was a body-aching mess. I was the worst kind of addict and I believed Aaron was the only one who could give me what I needed.

I had done endless miles of running over the last few weeks in a failed attempt to get Aaron off my mind. If I kept up my pace, I would end up blowing out my fucking knees.

I released a steadying sigh before I forced myself to roll out of bed. It was time to take another in a line of cold showers. Like all the other dreams I had about Aaron, this one had left my pussy soaking wet, and obligated me to finish myself off with my fingers. Masturbation got the job done, but it didn't come close to satisfying me like Aaron.

After a quick cold shower at three in the damn morning, I sat at my laptop and began to work on my latest manuscript. Beyond the mask of decency and benevolence I stayed hidden behind, I revealed to the world the dark side that lurked within me through my books, a twisted part of me that I've managed to keep well hidden. A part of me I had yet to understand. This part of myself scared the shit out of me as much as it excited me.

Aaron was one of a few people who saw my darkness, who I had allowed to see it. Infiltrating one of Florida's most dangerous motorcycle clubs was an idea that I'd contemplated for months after I moved to the area. If I was going to pull off something that dangerous and crazy and live to tell about it, I had to plan well.

Even with my planning, I never expected to get into the MC the way that I did. I never expected it to go that deep. I veered so far off my original course that I had to adopt a new one. Who would have ever believed that the August Knights would take me in, allow me to work for them, and allow me anywhere near the inner workings of their club? Twice, I was put in a position where I ended up with a gun in my hands and pulled the trigger both times.

Of all the obstacles I faced while working for the August Knights, nothing had impacted me like Aaron. I missed him so badly that I was tempted to do something as stupid as veer off my current plan and visit him again.

However strong my urges were for him, me returning to him was one thing I knew I couldn't do. I could never go back. If Aaron found out I used him and his MC and the true reason why, I was sure he would kill me. Knowing what I knew about him and how he operated, killing me was a certainty.

The idea of Aaron looking for me crossed my mind often now, but even if he searched for me, I'd put measures in place to keep myself hidden. He had no idea I was about four hundred miles away from him, right under his nose in South Florida.

I reigned in my ever-running thoughts of Aaron and proceeded to write the third installment of my motorcycle club series. The information I gathered while with Aaron's MC had given me ideas, insight, and so much material I had enough for a seven-book series.

The way I saw it, I did what any good investigative journalist would do. Sometimes, you had to go into the belly of the beast to get the answers you needed and the ideas that gave you the edge over your adversaries.

I was willing to do things that many others weren't willing to do. I was willing to take risks that others would never consider. If I didn't put myself out there, I would lose my edge. Losing my edge could mean death for someone with my jagged, dark past...a past that never stopped lurking. One I knew would never stop haunting me.

Chapter Four

Aaron

Another week and no fucking updates on Megan. I spent the week running guns and was forced to delay what I considered my most important task of tracking down Megan's lying ass. The longer it took me to find her, the more my rage against her grew.

The first place I decided to Investigate was the address on the driver's license. D hadn't found any new leads, and like me, he was called away on one of his field assignments.

So far, all D and I knew was that Megan Jones was not only the name Megan wrote her books under, it may have also been an alias to hide her true identity. It bothered the fuck out of me that I didn't truly know her. Facts were, she was as dangerous as anyone in my MC. The scariest part of the situation was that we never allowed an outsider to get that close to us. Megan could have killed all of us if she'd had a mind to do so and we wouldn't have seen it coming.

Since I couldn't sleep, I departed during the middle of the night and drove the long stretch from Florida to Texas. Exhausted, I slouched behind the steering wheel, but my mind was too restless to stop me from tracking down Megan.

A little after seven in the morning, I sat outside the office building of the woman whose address was on the driver's license. Before arriving here, I'd tried the home address on the license, but no one had answered the door. D had somehow linked the woman's home address on the driver's license with her place of business.

Going straight into investigative mode, I hadn't even bothered to check into a motel. Instead, I parked my truck across the street from the office building and fed the parking meter the change from my ashtray before I hiked across the paved street.

When people began to enter the building, I merged in with a group and followed them inside. Thankfully, this wasn't one of those buildings that had metal detectors and guards that wanted to see credentials.

A fresh, welcoming aroma met me as soon as I stepped far enough inside. The open floor plan allowed me to look up several stories to a giant tinted-glass ceiling. There was a coffee shop, a restaurant, and a few small shopping outlets on the first floor. You could glance up and on certain floors, see the large scripted letters that showcased the names of the businesses.

In the lounge area near the coffee shop, people sat with their laptops open while swiping at their devices, drinking coffee, and conversing. Their interactions with each other were loud and animated, no doubt, the caffeine doing its job.

The click of heels alerted me to a group of three women walking in my direction. Their conversations ceased as all three eyed me like I was a mouth-watering steak being prepared to their liking. I had shaved my beard off, so my face was cleaner and fresher looking, I presumed. To make myself more approachable, I pulled my hair back and secured it with a rubber band.

One of the ladies licked her lips suggestively, her eyes clocking every inch of me within seconds. One's eyebrows shot up as a gleaming smile spread across her face. The other just gawked, lips slightly parted.

Their pace slowed considerably the closer they got to me. Their heels scraped against the floor as they made an abrupt stop in front of me, halting my movement.

The group greeted me in unison like it was practiced. "Hello," they sang. Their greeting was followed by girlish giggles.

The brunette from the group asked, "Can I help you?" Her seductive tone and heated gaze indicated that she was offering the kind of help that could only be given behind closed doors.

After shaking my head no to the question, I greeted them with a quick, "Good morning," and zipped around them, quickening my steps to get away from them.

Clicking heels started up again, and their voices carried on purpose, I was sure.

"I'd like to help him all right. Right out of those clothes," one stated before they all giggled.

Another one of them expressed, "I'd like for him to help me out with something on my desk."

Their not-so-quiet banter made me smile. I was used to women treating me like I was a piece of meat. Therefore, I didn't feel bad about my tendency to fuck them once and leave them. However, it was too bad I was unable to apply that same principle to Megan's conniving ass.

The glass-encased legend on the lobby wall displayed that the Megan Jones attached to the address on the driver's license was an attorney who worked out of an office on the seventh floor. Could there be a connection that tied this Megan to *my* Megan?

As I turned to head toward the elevators, I was nearly trampled by another woman, and was hit with, "Hi, can I escort you to where you need to go?"

A lanky blonde with a blue business jacket and a short pink skirt that showed off legs for days had found her way into my personal space. The woman didn't hide her scanning eyes as they roamed my body from head to toe.

"Thank you," I said. "But, I think I can find my way."

She leaned in closely. I believed the woman was going to kiss me until I caught the flash of the business card she had pinched between her manicured fingers.

"You ever need anything, don't hesitate to call me," she offered, not the least bit ashamed that she was flirting with a perfect stranger, giving him an invite to her pussy as far as I was concerned.

I smiled and nodded before I took the card, being careful not to engage her in conversation so that I could continue with my mission. She hadn't even bothered to ask my name, which reinforced what I was to her. When I walked away, I didn't have to look back, I sensed her eyes all over me.

In jeans and a white T-shirt, I was likely the most plainly dressed person in the building, but people, especially *women*, often went out of their way to be nice to me.

With over fifty tattoos scattered all over my body, shoulder-length hair, and a darkly shadowed chin, I wasn't the kind of man a woman wanted to take home to meet her family.

However, I was the man a woman didn't mind having a one-night stand with; the one they didn't mind cheating on their husbands with or the one they didn't mind fucking in just about any location at any time.

At times, I didn't think they saw a person. I was a package. I was the epitome of the bad boy they fantasized about. I was the walking image of someone they wanted to fuck, and no matter what I did to myself: beard, no beard, short hair or long, I would never be the man they took home to their family or the one they wanted to marry. Shit, I wasn't even the one they would take out to a restaurant, and the idea of having a kid with my ass probably gave them nightmares.

I took the elevator up to the attorney's floor, hoping she would shed light on why someone was using her address and name as an alias.

My pace slowed when I walked into the highly fashionable and stylish-looking office. I glanced down at myself and around at the expensive paintings, the glossy floors, and highly varnished and perfectly finished furnishings.

"Can I help you?" the receptionist asked before my eyes made the full journey around the office space. Her wide smile danced under sparkling green eyes.

The way she bit the tip of her pen and eyed me insinuated she didn't care one bit about how I was dressed.

"I was hoping I could speak to Miss Jones," I stated in the most fake proper voice I could muster.

"She doesn't take walk-ins, but I can let her know that you dropped by. What's your name and why do you want to see her?"

I leaned over the receptionist's glossy granite counter, allowed my tongue to dart across my lips, and let my gaze travel over her body. If they were intent upon treating me like charbroiled steak, I may as well use whatever they saw in me to get what I wanted.

"I'm Detective Jeff Jackson," I lied while flashing one of the fake badges I used while hunting someone. "I was hoping I could see Miss Jones for just a few minutes about a suspect I'm tracking down. I'd tell you everything, but I'd have to get to know you better before I tell you all of my secrets."

My flirting had her blushing and grinning. The notion that I didn't have to try hard or come up with clever lines had me laughing on the inside.

"Don't go anywhere. I'll see if she will take you after her current client. She may have a moment to spare. I'll be right back."

The woman walked swiftly in the direction of her boss' office, glancing back at me with a wide grin the entire time. When she was out of sight, I dropped my smile and waited.

The receptionist returned rather quickly.

"Miss Jones said she'll see you, but only for a few minutes. I insisted that it was vitally important that she see you. She will be done with her client soon. You can have a seat, or you can stay here and talk to me."

"I think I'll take a seat because you look like the kind of girl that can get an innocent man like me into trouble."

She shook her head energetically and lowered her voice, not hiding that she was flirting. "I won't be any trouble. I promise," she said before placing the pen back at the corner of her lips and biting on it.

Her ringing phone saved me from gagging on my own words. As I headed to my seat, I glanced back at her on the phone and winked while she was handling her caller. She wasn't a bad-looking woman either. A sexy redhead with a nice small frame. The ring on her finger and the picture of a toddler between her and the man who was likely her husband I spotted displayed on her desk, revealed the rest of her story.

Less than five minutes later, another woman came strutting from the back. Her navy designer business suit was as expensive as everything in this place. Her gaze met mine and an immediate smile flashed across her face. She waved at the receptionist while passing her desk to head toward the exit.

The receptionist remained on her call, but she pointed me toward her boss' office, letting me know I could go back.

I cruised down the first short hall, which had an office on each side. Since none of the nameplates on the doors indicated Megan Jones, I turned down a second hall and found several offices back there, each with what must have been other lawyers.

The name of the place was Evans, Jones, & Carter, so Miss Jones was one of the partners. Miss Jones' office was located at the far end of the second hall. I knocked softly on her door and waited.

"Come in," she called.

When I stepped in, she stood, but her eyes were glued to a document in her hand.

"Have a seat, Mr. Jackson," she directed, but she hadn't glanced up yet.

I sat in one of the two brown leather chairs facing her desk and waited. Her office was as polished and sophisticated as she was dressed. Brown, black, and gray traces of leather were everywhere. Her desk was transparent, so I saw her black red-bottom pumps with a heel so high, it gave her at least five extra inches of height. She wore a red suit jacket, paired with a blue top that matched her blue skirt.

I never understood the need for makeup and those extra pieces and parts some women preferred. *Accessories.* This Megan flashed many parts from her expensive necklace and bangles on her wrist, to the broach attached to her lapel, the multiple rings on her fingers, and the dangling earrings.

I liked it when a woman kept it simple like *my* Megan. No makeup, her natural hair, and no extras. It allowed me to see a true depiction of a woman and not the polished trophy she transformed herself into.

Miss Jones finally placed the document on her desk and glanced at me. Her eyes scanned me quickly, much like the lady in the navy suit had. The lust peeking from the depths of her gaze told me she liked what she saw, but unlike the other ladies, she at least attempted to hide it under a layer of professionalism.

This Megan was nothing like mine. This one had a pale complexion with bone-straight dark brown hair and a model-slim frame. She was likely in her forties, but her heavy makeup and refined appearance had her looking in her early thirties. A small smile remained shining in her gaze, but it didn't spread to her lips.

"How can I help you?" she asked.

"I'm investigating a case that you may or may not have insight into. A piece of evidence in the case led me to you."

I had her full attention with those statements.

"I don't believe your personal or professional life has been compromised in any way, however, I am searching for a woman who is or was using your name and address as an alias."

Her smiling eyes grew tense, and her posture stiffened.

I handed her the driver's license to see if a picture of Megan would spark any knowledge.

"Do you know this woman?" I asked her, praying she said yes.

She shook her head as her eyes darted back and forth across the driver's license. Remaining quiet, she placed her fingers up to her painted lips, thinking.

Based on that lost look in her eyes, she didn't recognize who was in the picture. I would bet my next paycheck that this woman was chosen at random for her name.

I was wasting my fucking time chasing a dead-end lead. I slumped at the heavy weight of failure bearing down on my shoulders. Hopefully, D would be able to find me another lead because the hunt for Megan wasn't as easy as I anticipated.

The Megan that stood before me asked, "May I ask why are you looking for this woman? More importantly, why would she be using my information?"

"She stole something…" *My fucking heart.* "It was something of value that I'd like to get back. I believe your name was chosen at random."

Although Attorney Megan Jones and I exchanged numbers, and she made several calls to ensure her identity was protected, I was certain I would never see the woman again after this day.

Chapter Five

Aaron

I decided to stick around Texas for a few days. There had to have been a reason Megan used a Megan Jones from Texas as her alias. Was she from Texas? Was she currently in Texas?

The best of the roach motels would be my residence until I picked up a lead on Megan. I usually stuck out like a sore thumb inside the four and five-star hotels, so I didn't bother with them.

Just as I reached an elevated state of relaxation and my neck began to roll from sleep pulling me under, D's call sounded. I jerked my head up with a start and was talking before the phone reached my mouth and ear.

"What do you have for me?" I hadn't even said hello. D was used to my rugged demeanor and my usual aggravated tone.

"I dug until I found out where those centers are located that are receiving Megan's book sales profits. Someone paid good money to keep this shit hidden, but there's not much that stays hidden from me," D stated, chuckling. He wasn't being arrogant either. D had the ability to find shit meant to be buried and things that people assumed no longer existed.

"The money is going to two places in Texas. Grab a pen."

Although it had led to a dead end, I was glad I decided to follow up on the Texas address from Megan's driver's license. It meant I may have already made a trip I was likely going to have to make anyway. After reaching atop the wobbly desk at the foot of my squeaky bed, I found a cheap, flimsy pen.

"I'm ready," I told D, eager for another lead.

As soon as I scribbled the addresses and ended the call with D, I went to my truck and input the information into my GPS. Since it was only two in the afternoon, I decided to go and check out the locations D provided.

The first address took me to a place called The Kid's Club, which was something like a knock-off Boys and Girls Club. The Crestwood neighborhood wasn't the most glamorous environment, and I could tell right away that it wasn't a place you wanted to be stuck in at night.

Shabby and weathered buildings, littered streets, and graffiti-decorated walls filled my view. People hung out on the blocks, and I was sure they weren't hanging out because they were enjoying the sun.

I jolted forward and rocked back after slamming my foot on the brakes to keep from hitting a thin man who darted out into the path of my truck. The man was wearing a pink tank top and pale blue booty shorts holding up a flimsy cardboard sign that read, "Twerk it like you mean it."

I shook my head, attempting to rid my brain of the image I just saw. It was the kind of imagery that induced an early onset to erectile dysfunction.

The location alone should have been enough to stop me, but in my opinion, this place was nothing but a flip-side view of how I grew up in Copper County. However, in this area, I was the minority. I drove over the graveled parking lot of The Kid's Club and walked up to the building that should have been torn down years ago.

It was a brick building with burnt orange bricks missing from certain spots. Dirt was caked on a majority of the lower outside wall. The windows had bars that were breaking out of the crumbling bricks.

There were kids running around on the dirty basketball court located to the right side of the building. The nets on the basketball goals were missing, and nothing but the rusted rims remained on leaning poles propped up with sandbags.

On the far side of the building, I spotted sawhorses and equipment that indicated the outside of the building was in the process of receiving a long overdue makeover.

A floral fragrance that covered the scent of dust and mildew greeted me when I stepped into the building. A six-foot-two white man covered in tats in what I believed was a strictly black establishment had me sticking out like a big-ass neon flag. A few funny looks greeted me from some of the kids who walked by, but they didn't voice their comments if they had any.

Surprisingly, other than a few odd looks, no one stopped me from walking around observing as I searched for someone in charge of the place. Every room or open space was filled with toys, televisions, and computer stations for the kids.

Finally, way in the back of the building, I found a small office. The door was open, but no one was at the desk.

"Can I help you?" came a soft female voice from behind me.

"Yes. I'm Detective Mark Griffin," I lied easily. "I'm here on behalf of the Lincoln County Gang Unit."

I flashed my fake badge that the lady eyed suspiciously before I shoved it back into my back pocket.

She pointed me into what must have been her office. She had to turn sideways to get behind the tight space of her desk. She hadn't volunteered her name, but the nameplate on her desk said, Beverly Hudson.

She had a messy ponytail piled high on the top of her head. The air conditioning only produced enough cool air to stave off the worst of the heat, so her chocolate skin glistened with sweat. Like Megan, Beverly would definitely stand out in a crowd. It wasn't hard to keep eye contact with her, that's for sure. Her hazel eyes were in sharp contrast to her brown skin and forced you to keep your eyes on hers although it was easy to see she had a nice body.

"How can I help you, Detective Griffin?"

"We are trying to track down a woman that goes by the name of Megan Jones. She writes books under the same name, and a portion of the money from her books sales are routed to an organization that funds this facility. We are trying to find out who set up that fund since Megan Jones is possibly an alias not only used in her writing career but in her everyday life."

At the mention of who set up the funding, Miss Hudson failed to hide the fact that she'd become a little twitchy. She drummed her fingers over her desk as she avoided my eyes. And although I couldn't see it, I picked up on the sound of her leg bouncing under her desk.

"The fund was set up anonymously, so I know just as much as you do, *Detective*."

I wasn't sure if she even realized she had done it, but the way she placed a little extra inflection on the word detective indicated that she didn't believe my cover.

However, she continued without missing a beat. "The Phoenix Foundation distributes the money, but the donors remain anonymous. The foundation has been one of our sponsors since the doors on this place opened, and they never reveal to us who donates the money if the donor requested to remain anonymous. Their goal is to find us funding, and they are not legally obligated to tell us who the donors are."

She was lying and using useless information to distract me. When you were a part of the underworld like I was, with strategic training in detecting deception from the military, you could spot a lie a mile away. It was too fucking bad I couldn't tell when Megan's ass was lying, though.

Although I didn't probe Miss Hudson for answers, I fully intended to keep an eye on her.

After leaving, my next stop was to the other address D had given me. Much like the last place, this center was in need of more funding for the building fund as well. A group of kids pointed out Laura Parker to me, but I didn't approach her immediately. I took a moment to snoop around the center a bit.

Laura, unlike Beverly, didn't hide her disdain for me. Once she spotted me roaming inside her building, she stepped away from the group of kids she was talking to and approached me. She folded her arms over her small curvy frame and stepped in front of me, her sharp gaze cutting through me deep enough to reach my soul.

"Can I help you?" she asked after rolling her eyes so smoothly, I almost missed it.

I fed Laura the same story I gave Beverly Hudson, and Laura didn't even bother glancing at my badge when I flashed it.

"I don't know who donates the money and even if I did, lawfully, I don't have to tell you jack."

No amount of charm I believe I had would ever work on this woman. Laura was trouble, I saw it on her pursed lips, raised eyebrow, and on that I'll-fuck-up-your-world-white-boy expression she flashed me.

Laura Parker and Beverly Hudson weren't going to voluntarily tell me a damn thing. They were getting a substantial amount of donated money to keep the doors of their centers open, but neither woman claimed to know who the funds came from directly.

I figured I needed to stick around Texas for at least a few more days. My gut was telling me that Megan was somehow connected to these women or this area, and I would find out how.

Chapter Six

Aaron

The first thing I did was send Beverly Hudson's and Laura Parker's names to D to check out their backgrounds. It only took him a few hours to find out they had grown up in the Crestwood neighborhood on the outskirts of Houston, Texas.

Each woman had also spent time in the foster care system like Megan. Had they been her foster sisters at a certain point in her life or maybe friends? Had they gone to the same school?

D had also found an old address of Beverly Hudson's that linked her to the neighborhood. Although D gave me their personal address, I didn't believe I needed to visit Beverly or Laura at their apartment they shared because they weren't going to tell me shit.

The Crestwood neighborhood ended up being only miles away from the centers where the women worked. Could Megan have been from the neighborhood too? It was too much of a coincidence that money from her book sales supported the organizations these women ran.

Was I making too big a leap in thinking my Megan was connected to these women and this neighborhood? I didn't know, but my damn instincts were telling me to check it out anyway.

The black bill of my cap sat low over my eyes as I cruised down a block that resembled one of the hell-torn strips I had driven along when I was on deployment in Iraq. It was a bad idea, but I came to a stop in front of the dilapidated house of the address that D provided. It was Beverly Hudson's old address.

My plan was to see if I could find someone willing to volunteer the information, I knew I wasn't going to get from Beverly and Laura. Thankfully, I didn't see anyone that paid much attention to me as I approached the shot-gun-style house.

The flimsy outer door to the place had a screen on the bottom, but none in the top portion. You could stand on the weathered wood of the front porch and glance into the living room. The paint had peeled so badly off the outside of the house that you couldn't recognize the original color. The grayish color of the exposed wood was speckled with patches of mildew, and wild vines ran up the wood in certain areas.

The porch held two splintering rocking chairs, so worn they were likely one rock from falling apart. A ceiling fan hung over my head, wobbling and thumping with every turn. When I raised my hand to knock on the door, a woman, tall, slim, big eyes and puckered lips materialized out of nowhere.

"What you want, *white boy*?" She leaned her head closer to the opening in the doorway and took a quick peek in each direction of her block before glancing back at me.

"If the wrong person spots you, it's gonna be trouble for you. They'll crumble your cracka ass 'round these parts. I hope you got good sense enough to be packing?"

After I raised my shirt to ease her mind, her gaze landed on the .45 I had tucked in my jeans.

"Beverly Hudson or Laura Parker. Do you know either of them?"

"What the fuck you want with them? Beverly is my niece."

Based on her clipped tone this lady didn't care about me flashing a gun at her. If I meant any harm to her niece, she probably had somebody on speed dial that would come and take care of me.

"I don't want Beverly or Laura, but do you know if they had another friend they used to hang out with?"

She fished a pack of cigarettes out of her bra. Thanks to my height, I was flashed a view of her flabby dark brown tits. Her modesty was a thing of the past.

She eased a cigarette from the pack, retrieved a small blue lighter from deeper within her bra, and lit the cigarette all while I waited for her to answer me. She took a long drag from the cigarette as she eyed me out of the corner of her eye.

"That kind of information is going to cost you. We don't hand out information 'round here for free."

How the hell she was able to talk without smoke pouring from her mouth after the deep drag she'd taken from the cigarette was beyond me. Once she completed her statement, she twisted her bottom lip to the side and let the smoke shoot out in a long quick stream.

I understood how this world worked and had two crisp hundred-dollar bills waiting. I reached inside my pocket, eyeing her the same way she was eyeing me, and handed the bills over.

She jerked the bills from my hand and threw the cigarette back between her dry lips. I observed her eyes fly up in the air as she inspected the bills before slinging the raggedy door open.

"Come in 'fore somebody see you. I don't need nobody calling me a snitch."

She pointed me toward a chair as she sat on a worn brown leather couch before me. The leather of the couch resembled the dry wrinkled skin of an old man. Although her appearance suggested a woman in her late forties, this woman wore one of those old-lady gowns that my mother used to call a duster and a pair of those white plastic sandals like they issued prison inmates.

When I sat in the chair, dust flew up from either side of me. The chair was covered with one of those cheap, burnt orange, rug-type blankets. The place wasn't nasty, but it was dusty as hell, perhaps the dust coming in through that missing screen from the front door.

The woman didn't bother giving me her name although D already told me the house belonged to Violet Washington. She rubbed the bills between her fingers and raised them up again to make sure they were real.

She took her time about it too and didn't stop investigating the bills until she was sure about their authenticity.

"What you wanna know about this friend of my niece's?"

I had assumed as much, but this lady was confirming that there was a friend? Could that friend have been Megan?

"What's her name...*the friend*?"

"Bev and Laura only hung around with one other girl and that was years ago. They used to hang with this poor girl named..." she snapped her fingers, to help get the name out. Taking another long drag from that cigarette seemed to improve her memory.

"Daniels, yeah, her name was Lacey Daniels. The poor girl was being abused by her foster father and foster brother, and the crazy thing was they say the foster mother knew about it the whole time."

My eyebrow lifted, but I didn't comment. However, I locked the name Lacey Daniels in my head for D to investigate.

"Bev felt sorry for the poor girl and started hanging out with her. Anybody with half good sense could see that poor child wasn't being treated right."

My new informant put out her cigarette, tilted her head to the ceiling, and blew her smoke like an expert. Her upper lip was tucked behind her bottom one, leaving a hole for the smoke to exit.

"Do you know where they lived...Lacey and her foster family?"

The woman caught a chill that had her rubbing her hand repeatedly up and down her left arm after her body visibly shook. "Yeah, they didn't stay too far away from here. Over there in those Dumont Duplexes. But, after what happened over there, they tore the building down."

Now, she had my attention. I sat higher in the dusty chair.

"That poor girl must'a got tired of them people abusing her. I didn't see the crime scene, 'cause I was working that night and couldn't walk over there to be nosey."

The woman pointed; I suppose in the direction of the duplexes. "The place is right down the street, two blocks over. It ain't nothing but an empty lot there now. The kids claim that the lot is haunted."

This woman had no idea how much I wanted to stand and shake the information out of her. She was taking her time getting to whatever point she was aiming for.

Stretching out her pause, she scratched the back of her head, and her eyes remained on her feet before she went back into her bra and retrieved another cigarette. I winced at the sight of her tits that she didn't care one bit about flashing as she fished around in there for the small blue lighter.

Her story didn't continue until after she took two long pulls that took the cigarette down to the halfway point. I didn't know if this Lacey Daniels was the girl that might be Megan, but I needed to hear the rest of the lady's story.

"It's no wonder they tore down that duplex, the way they say that girl killed that family. Bev was fourteen at the time, so Lacey was probably the same age, but when I saw her, the time she came over here with Bev, she looked no more than eleven or twelve. She was skinny like her foster people starved her or something. Like I said, she must've got tired of that foster father raping on her because one day she just up and killed them all."

She fucking paused again, giving that cigarette every bit of her attention. This woman was killing my damn patience, stabbing it all to hell with her slow-ass storytelling. She flicked off the ashes of her cigarette into an already full ashtray.

"By the time I made it home that night, the yellow tape was already around that duplex and Bev came busting in this house out of breath, telling me that Lacey had stabbed them people up, killed every last one of 'em. She said the police found that lil' skinny girl in that house with the knife still in her hand, and she was all bloody. The kids say she looked like that Carrie from that Stephen King movie."

Another pull on that damn cigarette took it down past the butt where the ambers threatened to blaze if she sucked on it any harder. She shoved the butt into the ashtray with at least twenty others. Some of the ashes spilled over onto the scratched wood of her coffee table, but she didn't care.

"When the police finally got lil' Lacey out of that house of horror, they said that child had gone plum crazy. It's a shame for somebody that young to go crazy like that. When the news broke it down the next day, they say the foster father was stabbed over eighty-something times. The foster brother fifty-something times, and that old foster mother over fifty times."

Storyteller paused long enough to shake her head for cinematic effect. If this woman grew tired of sitting around her house smoking, she could try her hand at being a professional narrator.

"Come to find out, the cops found a recording of the father raping that little girl. The whole thing was some crazy shit. They say the recording the police found was so brutal that it justified the girl's actions. So, that poor child didn't break—she snapped clean in half. Ump. Ump. Ump."

Storyteller paused and shook her head with a far-off look in her eyes. The scene must have been a gruesome one if she was telling this story second-hand with that haunted look in her gaze.

"From what I know, they put lil' Lacey in the crazy house. After the way she had stabbed her foster family up, I don't know if she ever got out, even with the recorded evidence. If they did let her out, I don't know which way she went after that. Your two-hundred dollars' worth of time is up white-boy."

The smoking narrator glanced up, and as I expected, she reached her hand back into her bra. I cut my eyes in another direction. If she flashed her saggy-ass tits again, I was bound to get nauseated.

I stood, but paused before stepping away when it occurred to me to ask one more question. "What was the name of that foster family?"

"Them people kept to themselves. They didn't much talk to nobody outside their house. I think the father was Carlos or something that started with a C, and I never knew the son or mother's names."

"The family name?" I asked. "What was their last name?"

"Shit. I think it was something that started with a D, like one of them long Spanish names. They were Mexican or something."

If Lacey was Megan, what the hell was she doing with a Mexican family? The story was getting stranger by the minute.

"So, was Lacey Daniels a Mexican girl?"

"No. Back then, the foster care system didn't care nothing 'bout who they placed them kids with. Them damn case workers didn't have degrees and shit like they do now. I guess they figured that a little black girl with curly hair and light-enough brown skin wasn't too far off from being Mexican."

Curly Hair. That clue raised both my brows.

I pointed a daring finger at the storyteller. "If I check this story out, it had better not be a bunch of bullshit or I'm coming back for my money."

She shook her head vigorously. "Now, what reason I got to make up some shit like that? That shit was all over the news. All you gotta do is Google the shit or go to the library or something. They document shit like that."

Storyteller was right on my heels as I headed toward the door.

"Wait," she called from behind me, stopping me in my tracks. She walked up to and stuck her head through the opening in the door, glancing up and down her block. The sound of kids yelling grew loud and lowered with every passing second as the woman stood in the doorway, keeping me inside her living room. She glanced back at me and rolled her eyes. "I don't need nobody seeing you coming out of here."

She waved me forward when the coast was clear. I strolled past her taking quick steps, not bothering to render a goodbye greeting.

After I left the storyteller's house, I headed to where the duplex once was, and like she informed me, an empty lot sat there. Google didn't give me shit on what the woman claimed occurred at this address.

When I found the nearest library, their archived microfiche documents confirmed the story but didn't confirm Lacey Daniels' name. Since the girl was underage at the time, there were no pictures of her in the papers either. I couldn't find any pictures of the family she killed or their proper names.

My instincts were telling me the link between the friends, Beverly and Laura, who ran the organizations that were collecting funds from Megan's book sales, was too much of a coincidence for it not to be tied back to my Megan, who I was assuming was Lacey Daniels.

I wasn't done yet. I needed to confirm my suspicions and find clues as to where Megan was currently located and if she was, in fact, the teen who killed her entire foster family.

Chapter Seven

Megan

After reading the emergency text Beverly sent, my eyes slammed closed before my forehead fell into the palm of my unsteady hand. My finger jetted across the face of my phone, finding and pressing Beverly's number. She answered on the first ring.

"Are you okay? Is Laura okay?" I asked, breathlessly.

"I'm fine," she answered, tone calm. "Hold on a second while I dial in Laura."

Laura could hardly spit out the word hello before I asked several times if she were okay.

"I'm good, Megan. Calm down," she urged.

Her reassuring tone sent relief sweeping through my veins. Beverly and Laura were the closest people I had to family. As a matter of fact, they were the only family I was ever going to have. As far as I knew, my mother had handed me over to the state as soon as I was born, and my father could have been anybody.

"There was a detective that stopped by the centers earlier today asking after you," Beverly stated in way too calm a voice for the situation.

However calm the words were expressed, I began to twitch nervously as my leg bounced uncontrollably. My fist tightened around the pen in my hand.

"Bev, can you describe what the detective looked like?"

"Sexy as hell," she said with a hint of amusement in her tone.

"Really, Bev, was that all you remember about the man?" Laura asked. I could hear her irritation over the phone and could envision the crease Laura got in the center of her forehead along with that signature eye roll she'd perfected like an art form.

Bev continued, "Like I was saying before I was so rudely interrupted by the-man-police, this detective was tall and good-looking in a rough and rugged sort of way. Lengthy blondish hair, blue eyes, and lots of ink. The kind of guy that could make a woman do whatever the hell he wanted. He said he was from the Lincoln County Gang Unit, but I didn't believe him. I've never seen a police officer who looked like him before. Besides, I know more than my share of cops from when the kids at the club decide to do something stupid."

It sounded like she was describIng Aaron. "Did he have a beard, Bev?" I inquired, curious.

"No, no beard. He had that rugged look that women don't mind these days. And those eyes…those damn eyes spelled danger."

Although I didn't want Aaron searching for me, I prayed it was him who had visited my friends today. If it were anyone else hunting me because of my past, Beverly and Laura were in more danger than they realized. They were in denial, and always accusing me of overacting about the past. They never said so, or called me out for it, but I knew they believed I was delusional because I had spent time in an asylum.

"What did he want to know?" I asked, failing to put together the puzzle because I didn't have all of the pieces yet.

Laura chimed in this time. "He wanted to know about Megan Jones, the writer, so I don't think it has anything to do with the past. He wanted to know who Megan Jones *really* was and why we were receiving the profits from the sales of her books."

Laura sighed. "And I didn't think Mr. Detective was good-looking at all. As far as I'm concerned, they're all a pack of fucking rabid dogs."

Despite the upsetting news, I laughed along with Beverly at Laura's comment about men. She hated men. All of them.

"Are you sure that you two are okay?" I asked with a hint of laughter rumbling in my tone. "Did you check to make sure that no one is watching you or targeting you in any way?"

"We are fine, you worry too much," Laura stated. "Besides, you know I stay packing, so if a motherfucker stepped to me, he *will* be catching heat. And you will be happy to know that I finally got Bev to start carrying too, at least a .22. It might take a whole clip of those small-ass bullets to take someone down, but it's better than her bringing a knife to a gunfight."

Laura was the gangster of the group. She was a female with alpha-male tendencies. Laura was pretty, but to tell her so was the next best thing to insulting her. She dated only women and packed heat no matter where she went.

I was the quiet storm of the group…the sneaky one. I had an innocent face that fooled many but I had developed the ability to turn into a monster if necessary.

Beverly was the mediator, the voice of reason, the one who would urge us to think about our actions. Beverly was also the distractor of the group. She caught eyes no matter where she went. Everyone who knew her thought she was beautiful except *her*. She was teased so much when she was younger about her dark skin and curvy body that it left a lasting impression on her.

We'd all managed to live through and survive our own personal hells, so when we became friends, we formed a bond that would never be broken.

Beverly's voice sounded low in my ear. "Are you moving again? When are we going to get to see you again?"

At my insistence, we didn't speak freely over the phone line just in case we were being tapped. If I was preparing to move, Laura and Beverly knew it meant I was staying a step or two ahead of the ghosts of my past that had never stopped chasing me.

"Yes, I'll be moving soon and hopefully, I'll get a chance to see you two soon."

My jaw clenched tight with regret at the idea that I couldn't see the two people who meant the most to me in the world. Our visits were limited to once or twice a year.

"Is this shit ever going to end?" Laura asked. "How long are you supposed to run? Are you sure it's them, the…"

"Shhhh!" Bev and I hissed into the phone like vipers preparing to strike, trying to quiet Laura before she went on one of her cursing rampages and said too much.

Laura was used to speaking her mind, so having to talk in code and not being able to express herself was a punishment to her. If it were up to Laura, we'd likely be dead because she would have long ago initiated a war with an adversary I knew we couldn't beat.

"I have to go, ladies. Stay safe. And, Bev, please keep Laura out of trouble."

Their laughter sounded over the line, bringing an instant smile to my face.

"Love you," we all sang in one voice before we ended the call.

Someone was prowling around Beverly and Laura searching for me. Was it Aaron searching or had it been an investigator curious about what had gone down with my foster family many years ago? Bev and Laura weren't worried, but I didn't believe that they were as safe as they assumed.

Someone was hunting for Megan Jones. No one had ever hunted for Megan. It had to have been Aaron. If so, how had he found out that Beverly and Laura were receiving profits from my book sales?

My driver's license came to mind. I assumed I lost it, but Aaron must have found it or taken it. He did keep a suspicious eye on me before we started fucking every chance we got.

I forced ideas of sex with Aaron from my mind and concentrated. My driver's license would have landed him in Texas, but not at Beverly's and Laura's doorstep. How the heck had he connected those dots?

Aaron had expressed that he was the go-to guy for his MC when someone needed to be tracked down. Therefore, if he got it in his mind to find me, no matter how careful I believed I was, he would be determined enough to locate me.

The next number I dialed was the administrative office at my condo complex. After sitting through five minutes of the woman attempting to convince me to stay, I finally got the opportunity to speak.

"I will not be staying until the lease runs out. I understand that there will be a fee and I'm prepared to pay it."

She went into another speech about the benefits of staying. I sat thinking about where I would relocate to as I allowed the woman's energetic voice to carry on. Several places came to mind. The congested city of New York was one of them. Also, I'd been stubbornly avoiding the most logical move, which was to leave the United States altogether.

The long pause on the other end of the line drew my attention. I had no idea what the woman had said. "I'll come down in the morning to sign my paperwork. Thank you."

I hung up before the woman rolled into another speech. I had many more pressing things to think about than ending my lease early.

Chapter Eight

Aaron

Sleep eluded me. A whisper in the back of my mind kept telling me that I was on to something. This was the same edgy sensation that rode my bones when I tracked down people for the MC. I was close to something or on the right trail, I just didn't know the specifics yet.

I glanced at my watch that showed 2:05 a.m. It was the perfect time for me to return to those centers and see what Beverly Hudson and Laura Parker were hiding.

In all black, I crept to my truck and headed toward the centers. There may as well have been a damn block party going on outside the center Beverly ran. Teens, young adults, grown ass men and women, and even stray cats and dogs, all mingled.

The ear-splitting sound of loud music booming from the interior of cars that likely cost more than houses, filled the air as weed, alcohol, and all manner of illegal substances were being passed around.

Although the streets were alive with the sound of young heartbreak and the start of many nightmares, the center Beverly worked at was pitch dark on the inside and locked down. I pulled my cap low over my eyes and searched for a spot to turn around without hitting anyone.

The crowd was so amped up that groups and individuals danced and shouted over each other as one couple was one grind away from needing a condom.

I managed to turn my truck around without calling attention to the fact that I didn't fit in, not that some of them would have noticed me in their drug and alcohol induced states of mind.

As I left the scene in my rearview, I observed my surroundings with a keen eye to figure out the best way of getting into the center. My brakes squeaked as I slowed my truck to get a better look at a tight dark alley about half a mile away from the gathering.

The alley was wedged between a heavily barred pawn shop and a restaurant with a lopsided sign on the front that read, *Henry's*. The dark, smelly alley lined with overflowing dumpsters was the perfect spot for me to park my truck.

With nothing but a few tools and a small Maglite flashlight, which at the highest setting could outshine a headlight, I traveled back toward the noise of the crowd. To avoid being spotted by anyone, I ducked into a dark dusty alley a few buildings away from the center and hopped a fence to gain access to the center's back door.

A tethered wooden fence with missing sections and rotted wood separated the back of the center from the backyards of residences that I prayed didn't have dogs running loose.

When I visited the center earlier, I noticed the locks were deadbolt, which was good news for me. Bricks, bars, heavy locks, and alarm systems were not going to keep me out of a place if I wanted in. The military had dropped us in some of the most vicious places imaginable and left us to do whatever was necessary to survive. I became a professional burglar, an arsonist, a hitman, and even a fucking carpenter when it was necessary.

With a small tension wrench and a lock pick, I made quick work of getting the deadbolt on the back door open with my flashlight clamped between my lips. D had taken care of the toughest job of hacking into the security company's database and getting me the four-digit alarm code. Otherwise, I would have had to find and cut the alarm feed.

I eased the door open and closed it behind me as the alarm chirped with each passing second. After I entered the code, it gave a final double-chirp before going silent.

A half-hour search of Beverly's small office hadn't turned up a damn thing. I called D up, so he could talk me through hacking into her computer and emails, but the search ended in disappointment. Beverly's emails were clean from what I could tell.

Praying I would have better luck at my next stop, I left the center the same as when I entered it, resetting the alarm and securing the lock to the back door.

The area outside the center Laura worked at was in direct contrast to the scene I just left. The streets were deserted, and darkness enveloped the neighborhood, giving it an eerily skin-scratching vibe like danger lurked just out of sight. I drove past the center to find a place to park before creeping back to the building.

The sign outside the glass on the front door of Laura Parker's building said the center didn't open until seven o'clock. Since it was a little after five, I would have to make this search a quick one to avoid early arrivals.

Laura's office was as clean as Beverly's, but going through Laura's emails brought a smile to my face and had D chuckling on the other end of the line. The email files she hadn't cleared from her trash sparked my suspicions. When I began reading them, my jackpot radar went off.

One of her oldest, trashed emails confirmed that she was having an ongoing conversation with someone named Kelli Hunter about pretending to be the Jefferson Rehab facility. This was the same facility Megan claimed her sister was in. The same sister D was unsuccessful at finding information about. The only Jennifer's he discovered at that center were staff members.

Now this email was giving me yet another name. How many fucking aliases did Megan have? How many lies had she covered up?

Laura had likely been the woman my father talked to who provided Megan's alibi about her sister being in rehab. Why lie? What did Megan get out of infiltrating our MC? Why would someone knowingly place themselves in that much danger and not get anything out of it?

Her plan had undoubtedly been to get into our MC. What I couldn't fucking understand was why? I didn't know what piece of the puzzle I was missing. She hadn't outed us to the cops. Hell, she *couldn't*. She'd killed someone too.

It came to me like a flash of lightning had driven the idea into my brain. *Research!* Or could it be a sick fetish or type of devious gratification on her part? The crazy-ass woman had concocted this elaborate plan to infiltrate our MC to get firsthand knowledge of the internal workings and illegal activities of an MC such as ours. *No!*

I refused to believe that it was what Megan had been after. Knowledge? However, after we killed three men in my kitchen, she started talking about getting exclusives and writing and shit. She could well have devised this entire scheme in the name of research. The idea blew my mind wide open.

She'd even gotten to experience a few of our most sinful activities, participating in murder and burying bodies. We even had hot sex, with dead bodies as our audience. Was her mind that twisted? Was that why she wasn't the least bit shaken by the three dead men we killed in my kitchen?

Megan was a damn sociopath. More of Laura's emails supported my suspicions that the Megan I knew was the same person who killed her entire foster family when she was fourteen.

"Fuck!" My fists came down on the desk in an angry outburst of rage.

The bitch was crazy, so why the fuck did I still want to find her so badly? The sensible part of my brain urged me to stay as far away from Megan's crazy ass as possible. From the sounds of it, she likely had more skeletons than me.

How many other times had Megan done this? How many other organizations had she infiltrated in the name of research? How many people had she tricked to satisfy her sick, dangerous fetish? I believed the family she killed did a number on her mental state.

Time was running out, and D and I were only halfway through Laura's trashed emails. One of the emails asked Kelli about the weather, about if it was truly the Sunshine State as people said. The email was dated four days prior to my arrival in Texas.

At this point, I closed my eyes as my anger began to boil. There was only one place referred to as the "Sunshine State." Megan was right there in Florida. She was right under my fucking nose the entire time.

"D, can you check for Lacey Daniels, Kelli Hunter, or Megan Jones in Florida and see if these emails link back to any specific place in Florida?"

"I'm already on it," D answered.

***

Seven hours later and after much-needed sleep, D called me back. Hearing the hint of excitement in his voice was a good sign.

"I could only narrow the IP address to an area called Wavy Palms, but one of the emails mentioned something about Kelly shipping a MailEx package. Maybe you can see if you can get any information from one of the MailEx workers at the Wavy Palms location. Try a female employee, Knox. You have a way with them."

D laughed, causing a smile to creep across my lips. He and the rest of my old military squad had always teased me about the way certain women reacted to me. My smile deepened and turned into a sinister grin when I contemplated the lead D had just handed me.

I had no idea how D did the shit that he did, but as soon as I got back to my safe, I intended to send him a package to show my appreciation for his help. After I plugged the Wavy Palm's MailEx office into my GPS, I showered and prepared to get back on the highway to continue my hunt for Megan.

Hopefully, she was still in Florida. When I found her, I had no idea what I would do to her because uncovering her secrets had only heightened my anger toward her. She had landed herself in my danger zone, and it was not a good place.

Chapter Nine

Aaron

The face of my phone showed my father calling while I was driving back to Florida. All he wanted was to keep reminding me of how important it was to kill Megan for tricking us. Reluctantly, I swiped my screen and hit the speaker.

"Dad," I answered. I was not in the mood to listen to him right now.

"You got any leads on that tricky, little bitch? You were right about us not trusting her ass. She was good. I'll give her that much. That bitch could have killed every one of us, and I fell for her tricks. I want you to put an extra bullet in that black bitch's head for me. And I want to see the picture. Better yet, brIng me the body so I can shoot her ass again."

I'd been listening to this type of ranting since I revealed to my father that Megan had played us. He, like I, understood that it wasn't wise to share the news with the rest of the MC. Besides, he would have been too embarrassed to do so anyway.

We were the only ones who knew the depth of Megan's treachery. My job now was to find her and find out who the fuck she was and why she l went to such lengths to infiltrate us.

My brain refused to accept that she went through that much trouble for research. I cut into my father's rant, "I'm on my way back. It looks like she may be right there under our noses in Florida."

This bit of information set Shark off even more. He released what sounded like a mix of a snort and huff into the phone. "You mean that bitch is right here in Florida? If I knew where she was, I'd go and strangle her ass with my bare hands. And to think, I fucked that conniving little bitch."

At those words, I nearly lost control of my truck as I fought the steering wheel. The erratic movements sent my phone sliding across the passenger's seat. I reached across the seat, stretching my arm while struggling to keep an eye on the road. I gripped the wheel with one hand and held the phone up to my mouth with the other.

"You fucked Megan!"

"She tricked me. Seduced me. Used me to protect her from the rest of the MC. And my dumb ass let my dick do the thinking." My father's words were like acid eating through my eardrums.

My fucking brain was turning circles in my head as my father's irritating fucking voice drew on and on.

That's why he wouldn't say her name.

When she worked for us, he called her everything except Megan. I should have known it. The fucking biggest clue was there the entire time. My father had this stupid ass rule about not saying a woman's name again if he'd slipped and said it during sex.

That motherfucker!

My father's fucking voice came back through my phone, and all I wanted to do at that moment was punch his ass in the mouth.

"Let me tell you, it takes a real man to handle that kind of pussy. She would have fucked these young boy's heads up if I'd allowed them anywhere near her. After she shot Scud, it made these boys' dicks even harder for her, so she and I worked out a deal. I offered my protection, and the only payment I wanted was a taste."

Several deep breaths didn't calm the cloud of anger and rage that roared through me. My hands clenched around the steering wheel so tight, I could hardly keep my truck steady on the highway. The red sparks that clouded my vision right before I killed flashed across my view as pure unadulterated fury pushed through my veins and flooded my body.

I snatched my steering wheel and skidded off to the side of the road, going way too fast. The loud thrashing of rocks and a cloud of dust flew up into the air as I fishtailed my truck to a noisy stop. My truck bounced with a few loud hiccups before it came to rest.

When I asked Megan if my father had fucked her, she said...she fucking never gave me a straight answer. She told me my father had forbidden the MC from fucking her, but she never said anything about him.

"Aaron, you there?" my father asked, his infuriating voice projected loud over the phone. "You sound like you're having a fucking panic attack. I know you fucked her too. Could tell it the moment I saw you. Ain't no need to be ashamed of it. Shit, wasn't the first time I was with a black woman, but I'm certain it was yours."

My father's cackling laughter pissed me off even more. It wasn't that Megan was the only black woman I'd slept with, but that she was the first woman I allowed myself to love. Not only had she played my entire MC and fucked my father, but she had played a game with my fucking heart.

I was unsure at first, but now I had the ammunition I needed to put a bullet in Megan's head. My father's irritating fucking voice returned.

"That's why I forbid the MC to fuck her, son. Pussy so tight, I damn near had a heart attack. She would have had all of us thinking with our dicks. She would have fucked up all our heads. I mean, look at all the mistakes we've already made with her."

I knew his sneaky ass had ulterior motives for bringing Megan to my house. I cut into my father's rant, again. "I gotta go. D's calling me with another update."

Click.

D wasn't calling. I just didn't want to listen to him anymore. I closed my hand around my phone so tightly that I had to toss it onto the seat after hearing a low crack. My icy gaze panned the view before me, but I couldn't identify my surroundings because all I pictured was my hands around Megan's neck. Blazing fury coursed through my veins, and I intended to aim it all at the woman I now hated more than anything on this earth.

Chapter Ten

Megan

The last few days had been my most productive. I wrote over twenty thousand words. Now stretching before my morning run, I took in the beautiful beach less than a quarter of a mile away from my condo.

The neighborhood was runner friendly with its winding little running trails that circled the multi-million-dollar condos.

For nearly six months now, I lived in Florida including the month I spent with the August Knights Motorcycle Club. This was the longest I had settled in any place over the last three years.

I set a rule for myself that I would never settle in one place for more than six months. However, the people here in Florida were friendly and accommodating. Who was I kidding? Leaving Florida would take me away from my flirting desire to reconnect with Aaron's sexy ass.

Since September had rolled in, the slight drop in temperature produced the perfect type of weather for enjoying the outdoors. The breezy comfort was easily enjoyable. Today, the sun sat high in the sky, and the breeze off the ocean kissed my skin as soft sprinkles winded their way through the air and licked away the heat of the sun.

If it wasn't relaxing enough, the breeze never stopped sweeping my skin with its cool care. This was one of the most relaxing places I'd lived, but I had finally made the decision to move out of the country. I built up enough courage to leave the United States and would be moving to the Dominican Republic. Although I'd never been to the beautiful island, it was one of three places I'd chosen at random.

My turbulent past was the reason I moved around as often as possible. I also had a propensity for stirring up trouble, playing with fire, and throwing stones at hornets' nests. Despite my reason for doing the dangerous and disturbing things I got myself into, it often garnered me ideas and concepts for my books in the process. However, and more importantly, I gathered the knowledge needed in the art of survival.

I convinced myself that it was journalistic exploration, but the people I used in the process of gathering insight would find it highly insulting if they knew what I was truly using them for.

I inherited millions from my husband's death over three years ago. It wasn't until after he was killed that I found out his family owned seven of the most lucrative pharmaceutical manufacturing companies in the country.

My dearly departed husband, Eric Christenson, had kept the big secret from me. I often speculated on how he managed to take such good care of me on his military salary alone. Or how he could afford to take me on all those expensive trips? He didn't care about me traveling and spending months at a time away while he was on deployments. After his death, I found out he had ten million dollars in his trust fund.

He defied his family's demands for him to help run the family businesses and had joined the military instead. I met his family for the first time at his funeral, and despite the depressing event, they were cordial to me. Although I'd never officially met them before, they claimed that Eric had shared with them that he'd never been happier before his marriage to me.

When they called me the next week to meet them at their lawyer's office, I didn't know what to expect. Eric's last words were a love letter to me, and the last few sentences left my mouth hanging wide open. He'd left me every cent of his trust fund. The insane amount of money, ten and a half million dollars, didn't faze his family at all.

When you were sitting on endless millions, losing a little of it didn't hurt, I supposed. Eric's letter had also highlighted to his family that I wasn't aware that he had a trust fund.

My decision to settle down and attempt a normal life had eventually brought trouble lurking. It didn't matter that I called myself putting a number of protective measures in place. Several different aliases as well as living in seven different states before I decided I was safe wasn't enough. I had underestimated the determination of my enemies and if Eric hadn't died, I would have had to leave him to keep my past from eating him alive.

Living the life of a millionaire was fun for me—for about three months. When you discovered that there was only so much fun you could have with darkness lurking at your back, you tended to concentrate on more important things, like plotting survival strategies and escape plans. The inheritance allowed me the financial freedom to relocate my life on a whim, and the ability to run from any trouble I stirred up along the way.

I never had to work another day in my life, but I would trade every cent I inherited for a normal, worry-free life. Writing was always a secret hobby of mine. When you spent years locked away inside a nut house, you had to find an outlet or face losing your mind. Writing was also the one constant that kept me company in the lonely, nomadic, and sometimes dreary life I took on after my husband's death.

After a seven-mile run, I ignored the elevator and hiked up my stairs to my third-floor condo, making my legs burn a little bit longer before relaxing.

When I entered my apartment, a strange awareness overtook me—a sense that I was being watched. A distant view of the ocean met me after I walked over to my window and peeped out. I did the same at my side windows, which gave me a view of my neighbors in the condo complex next to mine. We weren't in high rises. The tallest building around the area went up to the fourth floor, giving the area a more laid-back look versus that of a city.

After my shower, I sat in front of my laptop and worked on my latest book again, but that sense of being spied on climbed onto my back and weighed me down. There were eyes on me. I sensed them and couldn't shake them.

I ambled over and stood at my bedroom window for a few long minutes. Was I being watched or was I being paranoid? My neighbor, Mr. Hancock, in the next set of

condos across the way, liked to people-watch through binoculars, but I couldn't see him. The couple on the fourth
floor were on their balcony. They were damn near fucking
each other out in public, so they didn't have time to put
eyes on me.

The nagging feeling of someone's eyes on me, lingered. I beat the sensation back. I was careful. I was safe.
I reminded myself. I was locked inside my condo, mind-
ing my own business. No one was watching me. It was my
twisted mind dredging up ghosts that weren't there. So,
why wasn't that feeling going away? Why couldn't I make
it go away?

Chapter Eleven

Aaron

It took less than ten minutes to get the information I needed from the lady at the mail delivery place. Initially, she had stuck to her guns about protecting her customer's privacy—even after I flashed her my fake badge.

After she saw Megan's picture, I was convinced she knew her or had at least seen her, so I used my bad-boy charm to pry the information out of her.

Thank God, I didn't have to use my dick on her. The woman was so sexually starved I made her cum in less than two minutes by dry rubbing her pussy through her panties after I reached under her skirt without her permission. It was a good thing I did it too because she knew Megan.

She didn't give me her address, but she provided the name of the condos Megan lived in, which happened to be only a few blocks and turns from the office location. The woman was kind enough to offer to go with me, and I didn't know if it was for concern for her customer or concern that she wouldn't see me again.

It took everything in me not to knock her out and tie her up. One, for making me finger fuck her for information and two, she was a loose end who could have warned Megan that I was searching for her. Before I stepped out of her office, I turned and reminded her about the date we had set in a few days—a date that I had no intention of keeping. Hell, I'd already forgotten the woman's name.

Hopefully, I would have Megan's ass and be gone by the time she realized I had no intention of going out or doing anything with her.

Hours later, I located Megan's condo, and I broke into two different condos to find the one that gave me the best view of Megan's. I hadn't seen her yet, but I was able to confirm that she lived on the third floor after flirting the information from the lady in their administrative office on the first floor.

My faked interest in the rental they had coming available had gotten me a sit-down with the manager. Thankfully for me, the woman, like most of the ones who presented a good-girl image, loved a bad boy, which, for me so far, had worked well in helping me find the woman I wanted to murder.

The third-floor condo I visited across a narrow street from Megan's provided the best view of not only her bedroom but a side view of her living room as well. Unfortunately, I had to tie up the older man who lived here. Hancock, he said his name was. I tied him to his bathroom sink so I could use his apartment to spy on Megan.

***

When I spotted Megan stretching for a run on the narrow street in front of her building that evening, every muscle in my body tensed and threatened to rip apart. Although murder had been on my mind for days, my finger stayed clear of the trigger as I spied on her through the scope of my rifle.

She was comfortable and relaxed like she didn't have a care in the world. She didn't look like the type of woman who would trick an entire MC and commit murder with no remorse.

Was she a serial killer, a sociopath, or *both*? Had she used us to further her writing career or had she used us to add to her body count? All I knew was that Megan was worse than any of us. A fucking female menace with a weapon we hadn't been able to fight against—her pussy.

She wore a pair of red and black jogging pants that stopped below her knees and highlighted that she had a fucking ridiculously fit body. Her sleeveless gray tank top matched her gray tennis shoes. The top stretched across her perfect tits and hung loosely at her small waist.

My tongue licked across my lips when she bent to stretch, and I cursed myself when my dick moved inside my pants. That short glimpse of her already had me getting hard.

It took me a moment to relax and think about how I wanted to handle this. What was I going to do to her first? I was thinking of torturing her before I killed her. I had only killed one woman to date, but *this one*? I could hardly wait to kill her for making my rage shoot to a whole new level.

Gripping Mr. Hancock's binoculars in one hand, I continued to spy on her through the scope of my rifle that I set up on the man's table. My spying gaze followed her as she took off on her run, and I didn't stop gawking until she was out of sight.

I stayed clear of the windows while maneuvering around the condo. These people pretended they weren't nosey, but they clung to those windows and balconies, spying at any little thing that moved.

I set up and angled my spying devices so that I could view inside Megan's condo from within the dark interior of Mr. Hancock's place. After sliding his couch into the perfect spot, I stayed within the safe zone to conceal myself from Megan's view. At the same time, the location allowed me to see her move around inside her place.

My scope gave me a view of her living room and bedroom. Sitting on the couch with the binoculars provided me a view of her living room, but an even better view of her bedroom.

I alternated between sitting behind my scope one minute and returning to the couch and binoculars the next as I waited on her. I remained undecided about how I wanted to handle her and this situation, so I relied on my patience and waited.

I eased up off the couch cushion when she entered her living room and trekked over to the table with the binoculars in my hand. After I placed my eye behind the scope, I pivoted my weapon around on its tripod to keep my eyes on her every move.

Sweat glistened on her golden-brown skin as she stepped across her living room stretching her arms. She stopped and turned in my direction like she sensed me watching her. The dwindling sun painted the sky a dim shade of gray that aided in keeping her from spotting me.

She took a step closer to the large stretch of windows that lined her living room and scanned the area outside her place. Again, her eyes stopped on me like she knew I was there.

Why the fuck hadn't I pulled the trigger yet? When she stepped away and entered her bedroom, I swiveled my scope to find her. She peeled off her top and reached for her pants. Like in the living room, she stopped again. Her fingers remained looped in the waist of her pants as she walked up to her bedroom window in her black sports bra. Her neck twisted in several directions, up and down before her gaze locked on the lens of my scope.

She sensed someone watching her. However, she had no idea it was the devil she'd pissed off. I should have killed her as soon as I confirmed it was her. But now, I was stuck watching her, unsure why I hadn't made a move yet.

After a while, she left the interior of her bedroom and entered what must have been the bathroom. I returned to the couch and remained there, waiting for her to return. The floor level of her building was slightly taller than Mr. Hancock's, so her third-floor condo sat a couple of feet higher.

I squinted into the binoculars, eager for the blurring lenses to focus before I missed something. She had on a pair of cut-off jean shorts and the points of her tits strained against the thin white top she wore. I continued to spy on her as she came right back to the window, blindly sensing me. She opened her curtains wider and turned back toward her bed.

She glanced back over her shoulder and smiled in my direction, proof that she knew she was being watched. I glanced around my area; sure she couldn't see me. The darkened interior of the apartment shielded me. I had positioned the couch up close to the window, but I'd done this on enough occasions that I knew how to position myself not to get caught. *How the fuck did she know she was being watched?*

This was the first time anyone had sensed me watching them. Maybe crazy people sensed other crazy people. It was also proof that she was not just the innocent writer she had presented. She was as much a predator as I was, but I had to remind myself that I was there to make sure she never preyed on anyone else.

Her wet flowing curls clung to her shoulders and neck. Her skin glowed with a just-out-of-the-shower, dewy mist. It irked me that I couldn't stop looking at her. Even as I wanted to kill her, my mouth watered to taste her on my tongue and make her cry out my name as I fucked her. She stared in my direction until her eyes stopped near where I was sitting.

I see you, you evil little cunt. You know that I'm watching you. Wait until I get my hands on your ass. My mind said one thing, but my fucking body did another.

Megan's eyes remained in my direction, but they didn't settle on me. What she did next set my blood to a slow boil. She sat on the edge of her bed, fondling herself as she continued to glance in my direction.

She spread her legs wide and let her hand slide over her pussy, fingering herself over her cut-off jeans. Her body moved against her fingers, giving me a show, making me hotter with every touch. My dick betrayed me again, hardening when she let her hand slide between her legs.

Her busy fingers popped the button on her shorts and slid the zipper down before she slipped her hand inside. As she played with herself, she adjusted her eyes so that it appeared she was looking directly at me. After extracting her glistening fingers, she licked them with a deliberate upward stroke of her hot tongue.

When she scooted to the edge of the bed and lowered her pants, my breath hitched before my tongue slid across my lips. I shook my head, hoping she wasn't about to do what I thought she was about to do. She turned her back to me as she worked her shorts down, giving me a good view of that plump, sweet ass of hers.

Positioning herself back on the edge of the bed, one of her legs dangled over the side, and the other stayed atop the bedding, spread wide enough that I saw parts of her tempting pussy behind the sheer purple underwear she wore. Her middle finger snaked up her stomach before she slipped it into her mouth and licked it, getting it wet and ready.

Once she made a show of licking that finger, she reached down and slipped her panties to the side. She spread her lower lips so that I saw the pink inside her pussy. I salivated at the sight and couldn't swallow fast enough to stop the flow. So much blood raced to my dick, I was afraid it might explode.

While her pointer finger and ring finger spread her pussy open, she let her middle finger circle her clit. At the sight of the visual stimulation she showcased, I couldn't stop my hand from sliding over the hard line of my dick.

When she slipped her middle finger inside and rolled her body against her hand, my dick throbbed, and lust consumed me. I wanted nothing more than to go over there and fuck her brains out, but I was not ready for her to see me yet. I hadn't come up with a solid plan on how or where I would take her to torture and kill her.

She extracted her finger and now had two fingers snaking up her stomach and making their way to her hot wet tongue. God, her tongue and soft lips had felt so damn good sliding up and down my dick. It was so fucking wet and hot. She knew how to use that dirty, quiet, little tongue of hers so well. I ached to have it on any part of my flesh now burning with desire as I was unable to look away.

She sucked her fingers as her pussy danced for me, glistening with her wetness. She reached down and massaged her clit before sliding in the agile fingers she'd wet. The sight of such a sinful display made my dick jump in my hand. I couldn't control my breathing anymore as I undid my belt, button, and zipper with quick, anxious movements.

I reached into my pants and gripped my dick, no longer able to just watch. Her actions had depleted my resolve to resist her tempting show. Precum slipped from my tip as I stroked my dick—watching her, watch me, as I fantasized about being inside her tight walls.

I got a much better view of how well she was fingering herself when she spread her legs wider. Her middle and ring finger worked in and out of her pussy faster as she twirled her body in a way that flashed the top and bottom view of her. She worked herself closer to orgasm but stopped abruptly to let three fingers slide up her stomach. I knew what was coming next and started stroking my dick faster.

Repeating her actions with three fingers, she licked her juices from the one's she'd wet, making me want a taste. I would have liked nothing more than to feast on her. The idea of it made me sink my teeth into my bottom lip after my tongue slid across it.

When Megan eased her fingers out of her mouth, she sent them back on the journey to explore herself, and I released a deep exhale as my eyes widened in excitement. She shoved those three wet fingers into her pussy, working them in and out. It took everything in me: willpower, determination, and drive, not to cum on the spot or get up and go over there.

My dick was so hard it ached, and all I could do to calm it was stroke it faster when she started thrusting and moving faster.

She was close. I saw it when her body began to shake and in the urgent drive of her fingers in and out of herself. I couldn't take it anymore. Her lush lips fell apart while she fucked herself wildly, and I lost it.

Watching her cum had gotten me there as a stream of cum shot out and landed on the floor before me. Another hot shot sprayed all over Mr. Hancock's couch. Some even drizzled down my fingers as the fucking binoculars shook in my trembling hand because I refused to let them drop away from the sight of *her*.

Megan let her head fall back as she continued to stroke her pussy, so wet at this point, I noticed that her juices had dripped down to her pale blue spread. She sat there staring at me before she got up and snatched her curtains closed.

I let the binoculars drop from my shaking hand, but my semi-hard dick remained wrapped in the cupped fist of my other hand. My urge to fuck Megan grew so intense, I had to close my eyes and meditate to get my breathing back under control.

I pictured the storyteller's droopy tits, hoping that image would calm me down, but it didn't work. All the images of Megan fucking herself flooded my brain and caused a massive amount of lust to continue to course through me.

This was an embarrassing first for me. First, I failed to kill my target. Then, I sat there like a highschooler and got off on watching her fuck herself. Now, my fucking body and mind were in a battle over the next move I would make.

It took much more than meditation to get my dick to stop throbbing. Not even the idea of how she'd tricked me, or my MC had gotten me under control.

For once, I agreed with my father. "She's fucked my head up," I mumbled to myself before slamming my eyes shut. I struggled to concentrate on why I was truly there because the last thing I wanted to do right at this moment was kill her. All I could concentrate on was how good it would feel to fuck her.

Chapter Twelve

Megan

Maybe I shouldn't have gotten myself off in the window like that because I couldn't stop thinking about Aaron. Shit, my crazy ass even imagined it were him watching me. Instead, it was likely creepy old Mr. Hancock.

His old butt probably got off on watching me. I may have even given his ass a heart attack.

Since he was so damned nosey, he damn sure saw a hell of a lot of me and was likely on peeping-Tom overload after my scene.

A cool shower after my display and writing until my fingers ached hadn't done any good to help me sleep. I couldn't find peace. My nerves were on edge, and an air of paranoia that had been riding me all day intensified. I couldn't stop peeking out of my damn windows.

I was glad I planned to move because every time feelings consumed me like this, something crazy happened. After peeing and washing my hands, I sat on the edge of my bed. Memories of Aaron plagued me. His face flashed across my mind and caused my nipples to tighten and my pussy to throb with a level of expectancy that wouldn't be satisfied. Goosebumps rose on various parts of my body at the phantom touch of his hands stroking me.

The man had a fucking hold on me that I couldn't shake. When I was with him, he had me open for him so badly I was ready to do all types of sinful sexual acts.

My gaze traveled through the dark and found my laptop, but I decided I didn't want to start writing because I wouldn't stop until daybreak.

Instead, I strolled through my dark bedroom and headed for the kitchen. I didn't bother turning any lights on because I knew the place like the back of my hand. Most nights, just sitting in my bed or in the living room and staring out at the moonlit view was enough to calm me whenever my body begged for Aaron. Maybe a nice chunk of cheesecake would settle me down and give me that empty-calorie, false happiness vibe.

I gripped the refrigerator door with one hand and reached in and picked up the slice I hadn't finished with yesterday's surf-and-turf dinner I'd prepared.

I closed the door to the refrigerator and jumped about as high as a cat on a hot tin roof. The container in my hand dropped to the floor. My heart thundered in my chest as my eyes adjusted to the dark figure standing only feet away from me.

When I processed who was standing in my kitchen, my body seized. I would have likely pissed all over myself if I hadn't just used the bathroom. I stood there frozen, a million questions running through my brain.

Afraid didn't describe my state at this moment. Panicked and terrified weren't strong enough words either. The crazy shit I pulled with the August Knights Motorcycle Club had doubled back to bite my ass off. I was sure that I covered my tracks well, but I'd apparently not covered them well enough.

I believe I was able to pull the stunt off with the MC because I finally accepted that I was more twisted than I'd originally led myself to believe. It was like I needed the fear. I needed it like normal people wanted excitement in their lives. However, the level of excitement I craved crossed the line and swerved over into the crazy zone.

I realized that I truly hadn't experienced true fear of anyone in the MC until I'd glanced into Aaron's eyes for the first time. There was a depth to his darkness that had rung alarm bells within me, letting me know that no matter how crazy I believed my ass was, his ass was crazier. No matter what I had seen, he had seen worse. No matter what I had done, he had done worse.

I'd witnessed Aaron kill. I remembered that dead look he got in his eyes that told me he didn't feel anything when he took someone's life.

Since he was here in my kitchen, he'd figured out I had tricked him and his MC.

"Are you here to kill me?" The question fell from my lips in my normal, easy tone, which was the exact opposite of my current panicked state. My damn insides were threatening to shake out onto my kitchen floor.

The cool ceramic tile under my bare feet was all that kept me grounded. My fear grew so strong, I wobbled, attempting to keep it contained.

Aaron answered my question by lifting his gun. Without shoes, I was eye-level to the top of his chest, so his outstretched arm had the gun leveled with my head.

The silence between us, and the barrel of that gun pointed between my eyes made the air in the room freeze. My erratic, adventurous, and often dangerous tendencies had finally caught up with me.

For a while, I believed I was suicidal, but I'd aimed a gun to my head before as well pressed a razor to my wrist, but I could never follow through. I enjoyed living enough that it confirmed my being suicidal wasn't one of my problems.

The few therapists I saw recited to me in medical terms that I was a few steps from being insane. They hadn't outright said the word insane. Instead, they used proper medical terms that made the word insane not sound so bad. Like psychotic break, mild psychosis, or disambiguation of the mind.

Maybe I was a functionally insane freak, but if I was insane, what did that make Aaron? *Fuck!* What did it make me for having feelings for him? Feelings I'd denied until I found myself dreaming about him and remembering all the time we spent with each other. The way we were caressing and asking after each other. The lingering kisses. All of the hugs and cuddling.

Now, my shaky legs barely held me up as I faced him. My eyes never wavered from the steady hold he had on the raised gun. The darkness kept me from seeing the full view of him, but his presence ignited the dark space of my kitchen with sparks of pure terror.

I was sure Aaron had feelings for me when I lived in his home for those two weeks. He gave me the best sex of my life, and we could never seem to get enough of each other. He told me I gave him the same in return. Maybe it was the reason he hadn't pulled the trigger yet.

The idea that he might still have feelings for me urged me to move stupidly closer to him. I inched close enough that I had to tilt my head to avoid stepping into the gun he hadn't lowered yet. His beard was shaved off. However, even in the dimness, I'd be damned if he didn't look more tempting than I remembered.

When he lowered the weapon, his movement sent a few splashes of light over his face. He stood, fuming with his eyes dead locked on mine. The veins in his neck and forehead bulged, and his jaw was clenched so tight the bone was threatening to break through the skin.

I could literally feel the anger rolling off his body. His breathing kicked up a notch, but he didn't say one word, nor did he back away as I inched closer to him and placed my hand against his swelling chest right over his heart.

My gaze never wavered, and although it was dark, I glanced right into the depth of Aaron's icy stare. His face remained pinched with a fury that I could not only sense, but feel it bounding off his body in angry waves.

"After you kill me, then what are you going to do? Will you pour acid on me and throw me into a deep dark hole?"

His shoulders dropped a hair. It was the first real re-action he'd shown me. His face remained contorted with so much anger, I hardly recognized him.

He shoved me. No warning, only the strong force of his hand pressed against my chest. The action caused me to stumble back a few paces as I fought to maintain my balance. The quickness of his action stunned me, and I stared, wide-eyed at him.

The clink of his gun sounded when he reached back and sat it on the counter behind him. Then, like before, he delivered another hard shove that sent me back and into the wall hard enough for the quick breath I'd sucked in to shoot out of my mouth.

Aaron didn't give me time to catch the breath that I lost because his broad muscular body was standing over mine. His strong arms rested on either side of my head, the same way he had stood over me inside his pantry that first time.

His harsh breaths whipped through the air and lifted a few strands of my hair that had escaped my messy ponytail. His face inched closer to mine until his lips sat inches from my shocked, parted ones. His breaths washed over my face and mingled with my own labored breathing. We stood in an area where the moonlight cast away most of the shadows, so I could spot the deadly gleam that shone in his eyes.

"I'm going to fuck you first and then I'm going to kill you. Or maybe I'll kill you while I'm fucking you. I haven't decided yet." His words were calm, even, low, and in direct contrast to his actions.

The voice in my head screamed for me to bolt, to duck under his muscular arm and run like hell, but my fucking body refused to move a muscle. The idea of sex with Aaron had me buzzing with crazy lust.

There went my answer. Only a fucking insane person would choose sex over their life.

He placed his left hand on the center of my chest while the right one slid down my stomach until he caught the waistband of my pajama shorts and my panties and yanked them down in one fast sweep.

I even helped him a little by lifting my feet and flinging my legs to kick the bottoms off.

The sound of his belt coming loose and his zipper sliding down registered. He shoved his pants down enough for his dick to pop out. It was heavy against my stomach, sitting there like a hot, flesh-filled weight.

Aaron had a fucking beast. There was no other way to describe it. He alone shattered every stereotype mentioned about certain men having small dicks. Aaron had about ten thick inches.

The first time I saw it, I paused and contemplated if I was brave enough to tackle his shit. However, I learned from experience that he knew how to use his dick well enough that he'd have you ready to sell your first born to have it inside you just one more time.

Hell, I think I was possibly trading my life for a hit now. Instead of running for my life, I anticipated how good it would be to have him inside me. He was so hard; he could cause bodily damage if he took me the way his anger was suggesting he might.

He lifted 97ffortessly and drove his hard dick into me with such force, I just knew he'd driven me through the damn wall.

A moment ago, he told me that he would kill me. He killed me all right; with his dick shoved so far up my pussy he had knocked the oxygen out of my lungs.

The sweet pain and the sinful pleasure overtook me, and my twisted mind didn't know whether to scream or moan. I think I did a little of both.

He paused for a second, I suppose to gather himself since he was breathing as hard as me. He started powering strong thrusts into me so that my ass knocked against the wall hard enough that I knew it would bruise. He was rough before, but this was brutal, and I fucking loved it.

I loved it so much that I found a way to get my legs wrapped around him, which sent his hard thrust upward. My body inched up the wall with every thrust, likely knocking the pictures off my neighbor's walls. I had a tight grip around his neck, holding him to me as he pounded me into orgasmic bliss.

"Aaron, oh God!" I screamed so loud I believed I scratched one of my vocal cords. I couldn't breathe or think. Having his dick buried inside me elicited a delicious commotion that sparked within the depths of my body. It was glorious. It was magnificent. I couldn't believe I'd had enough willpower to leave *this* behind after he asked me to stay.

His loud roar echoed throughout my kitchen as he filled me with so much hot cum it dripped down the inside of my thigh.

We stood there, breathing hard, connected to each other for what seemed like an eternity. When he realized he still hated me, he flashed a frown before pulling out of me and letting my feet drop to the floor.

"Put some fucking clothes on," he growled. "You're coming with me. If you try anything, I'll make you watch me kill your neighbors just for pissing me off."

I tipped my head once and moved swiftly, blazing a frantic path toward my bedroom. My wet pussy and ass were going to have to air dry because I had enough good sense to obey his request and hurry the hell up.

When I noticed he hadn't followed me into my room, I stepped into the bathroom and wiped myself down with a wet soapy towel before I headed toward my dresser. As I picked up a clean pair of purple panties to put on, he stood in my doorway clocking my every move.

As a testament to him, every pair of panties I owned now were a different shade of purple because it was the color he said he liked on me.

As turned on as he had me only moments ago in the kitchen, I was equally as frightened of Aaron now. My frantic fingers fished around in my bottom drawer until I found a loose pair of khakis and a T-shirt to throw on over my sleep-tee. I quickly threw on a pair of socks and my best running shoes, in case I got away and had a chance to run.

"Pack some shit. I haven't decided how long I want to torture you for before I kill you," he said while his body filled my bedroom doorway. The gun was back in his hand.

Unable to drink my fear fast enough to function properly, my body trembled as I fumbled with my clothes and personal items. I dropped more items on the floor than I was stuffing into my backpack. Maybe the doctors had gotten it wrong. Maybe I wasn't insane. If I were, I wouldn't have good enough sense to be scared right now, right?

Jeans, sweats, T-shirts, panties, and bras were shoved into my backpack. After jamming the items in, it took effort for me to get the zipper closed.

I aimed my thumb toward the bathroom, and Aaron nodded, understanding that I needed something from there. After I ran in and grabbed my toiletry bag, I slung my backpack over one shoulder.

When I reached for my purse, my hand halted at Aaron's angry words, "Leave it!" I was too terrified to look in his direction. "You're not going to need a purse where you're going."

Those words took my breath and left me standing there frozen. He turned out of my doorway and marched away.

That confirmed it. Aaron was definitely going to kill my ass. Now, I was faced with finding a way to make him do it faster. It was the only sure-fire way I wouldn't suffer. I wasn't afraid to die. I just didn't want to endure the suffering that sometimes went along with meeting death.

I followed Aaron with hesitant steps. How would he do it? Where was he taking me to kill me? Thankfully, I snatched my cell phone off my dresser and shoved it into my backpack along with my clothes.

Maybe my twisted mind had imagined he felt something other than lust for me. Maybe he took pity on me because he knew I was crazy. Since he made me pack a bag, I assumed he planned to take me away from Florida. Probably to that Tennessee cliff he ditched Chuck's truck, so he could throw my body over those jagged rocks and watch as I disappeared into that dark water below.

When I stepped into the elevator with Aaron, the blood in my veins stopped flowing. The only sound I heard was the loud *thump* of my heart pounding in my ears.

More of my sanity was returning because the voice in my head kept yelling for me to run. And run was exactly what I did when the *ding* of the elevator sounded, and the door opened.

The thundering of my feet beating up the lobby floor and my harsh breathing projected loudly as I attempted to escape Aaron. I had no idea how he did it, but Aaron ran me down so fast I hardly got a good stride going.

He yanked me back to him by my backpack so hard that I turned and smacked into his hard chest. The impact against his firm body knocked the wind out of me, making me cough a few times.

"What the fuck did I tell you, Megan? Do you want me to kill more people than I have to?"

His angry gaze rained down on my wide eyes staring up at him. I shook my head and fought to send air into my starving lungs.

Because of the late hour, there was no one in the lobby that could help me, and it would be as deserted outside. I knew from the many sleepless nights I endured that the two security guards who were supposed to be on duty showed up at the start of their shift and didn't return until the last hour of their shift the following morning.

"Scream, and I'll give you something to really scream for," he said as his wild eyes bore into mine.

Aaron chaperoned me to the passenger's side of his truck and assisted by shoving me into the front seat once

I climbed far enough into the cab. I straightened myself out after landing on my elbow.

I tossed my backpack into the back seat and scanned the interior of the truck for a weapon as Aaron made his way around the front of the truck, his angry eyes locked on mine. He hadn't lost that rigid posture from the lobby and his face remained pinched in anger.

Did he expect me not to fight for my own life? The next chance I got, I planned to run again. Without an ID or money, I would have a hard time making myself disappear. *If* I was lucky enough to get away.

Chapter Thirteen

Megan

The silence that filled the cab of Aaron's truck taunted me. It was a form of nonverbal abuse. For at least a half hour, the roar of the engine and the constant whirl from the truck's air conditioner were the only sounds. Aaron was a naturally quiet man, but the tension in the truck was thick enough to suffocate us.

My twisted mind only processed one plan for my survival—*run!*

Seething hatred filled each glance Aaron sent in my direction. I sensed the agitation in his silent movements without glancing his way. I lurched with a start at the sudden roar of his incensed voice.

"I never did believe that bullshit story you told about your crack-addicted sister owing the MC money. I sensed from the beginning that you had another agenda, but I could never figure it out because you were too busy drowning me in pussy. Please tell me you didn't play my entire MC for some sort of sick entertainment of yours."

Clueless as to what to tell him, I didn't render an answer. Maybe I truly was insane for what I'd done, for what I'd been crazy enough to do. The instant I believed I could get away with something so outrageously stupid as infiltrating the August Knights, my mind started easing into the plan, and I'd enjoyed the ride along the way.

Wait. I didn't drown Aaron in pussy. As I recalled it, he was the one who approached me, practically demanding my pussy. Of course, I couldn't say what I was thinking out loud since Aaron now hung something as serious as my life over my head.

"I'm sorry," I choked out, keeping my gaze straight ahead.

"Sorry doesn't mean a damn thing. You could have killed us all. You could have gathered intel and given it to our enemies. You made a fool out of us. You'd better be glad it's only my father and me who know what you did because you could have twenty of us on your ass instead of just me."

I remained quiet and unsure as I listened to Aaron's angry words. He previously revealed to me that he was the one the MC usually sent to track people down whenever they needed someone caught or killed. I should have heeded Aaron's words, packed my shit, and moved away from Florida like I planned to in the first place.

"You're worse than we are. I heard and read about what you did to your foster family in Texas, Megan. Or should I say, *Lacey Daniels*."

Hearing my real name brought back so many horrifying memories, it made my stomach roll. Closing my eyes, I concentrated on anything but Texas. What had happened in Texas was what had broken me. It had turned me into this person who needed danger to live. Not only that, I believed I needed danger to survive.

There were times, when I wondered if my mind had gotten so twisted that I made myself believe someone was chasing me. Texas had turned me into a freak, and Aaron was right. I was worse than him and his MC.

"After reading how you hacked that family up, I was thinking that we should have been the ones afraid. In my kitchen, you got off on killing Chuck and seeing me kill Dutch and Clint, didn't you?"

He continued without giving me a chance to answer. "I knew something was up when I found you stooping over the dead man's body, observing your handiwork. It was what you wanted the entire time. You were searching for the right marks that could bring you the death you craved, the kind of destruction you lived for. Why didn't you kill me, huh? Why the fuck didn't you put a bullet in my fucking head?"

The sharp sting of tears peppered my eyes. Was Aaron's description of me accurate? Was I truly that fucked up?

"Answer me, goddammit!"

Aaron's thundering voice nearly drove me out of my skin, but his side-eye glare said I needed to answer him.

"I didn't want to kill you or any of your people. I only wanted to see how you lived, even if it meant me witnessing you killing people. I wanted to observe others that live in dangerous situations to see if I could figure out what is wrong with me. Nothing has helped me. I'm fucked up, broken, twisted in so many ways, I can't unbend myself."

"So, we were your test subjects? Nothing more than human lab rats to you?"

The loud boom of Aaron's hand slamming into the steering wheel caused me to claw at the door panel.

"Why the fuck did you pick *us*?"

Although the door was locked, I gripped the latch and remained pressed against it.

Aaron's gaze was the worst I'd seen so far. Death darkened his eyes, and his body sat in a tense hunched position as he fought to hold in a sea of rage that demanded to be let out.

"And you fucked my father. I asked you, outright, if my father fucked you and your clever ass avoided the question. Was it a thrill for you? Some type of freakish conquest? Fucking father and son?"

Based on how tight Aaron's skin stretched against his knuckles as he gripped the steering wheel, I didn't have to guess that he wanted nothing more than to strangle me with his bare hands.

I clamped my lips shut because my words weren't doing shit but pissing him off more.

"You'd better fucking answer my question, Megan or Lacey. I don't even know what the fuck to call you."

It was difficult, but I swallowed the baseball-sized lump in my throat and answered him.

"It was the only way to get him to protect me from the rest of the MC," I said, my voice low and shaky.

Looking back at it now, I wasn't sorry I'd slept with Shark. I naïvely assumed that a group known for being racist wouldn't want to touch me sexually with a ten-foot pole, but I couldn't have been more wrong.

When I discovered that the group didn't have a problem sleeping with an African American woman, the quick fix was agreeing to sleep with the only man I knew with the power to protect me. My moral compass had clearly been destroyed along with my sanity, so sleeping with one biker versus the entire crew was the most logical decision my brain could make at the time.

Aaron reached over and groped me roughly between my legs, jarring me, snatching me back into our tense reality.

"Why stop at him and me? Why not go for the whole MC? Wasn't that what you wanted, to get fucked? To fuck us and laugh at us after you got what you wanted? I fucking hate you!"

His violent voice grew quiet as his heavy breaths filled the cab of his truck. His nostrils flared like he was preparing to breathe fire.

"Now that I know what you are about, I'm going to fucking make you pay. I'm going to make you suffer. And your friends, your partners in crime, Beverly and Laura, you're going to have to have closed-casket funerals. I killed those bitches. I let them each know that it was *you* who brought death to their doors."

My head whipped around at Aaron's deadly revelation. "No!" I screamed; my voice ripped from a place deep inside my chest as tears streamed down my face. My sobs escaped uncontrollably, as agonizing hiccupping cries scratched my throat.

I killed them. Knowing that I caused the death of the only people who looked out for me was a fate worse than death itself. Beverly and Laura had helped me escape a situation that would have otherwise killed me.

"So, the she-devil does care about someone?" Aaron's taunting voice sank me deeper into my despair.

"I took pictures of them for you. Figured you'd like to see more gruesome acts of death. Use that shit in your books. Now, I understand why those damn books are so good. Everything in them is probably shit you've manipulated your way into seeing or have done yourself."

I descended into a haze of despair so deep, Aaron's words faded into the background. I fell against the door, shaking and crying with my head hanging low to my chest.

My heart had stopped beating and blood was no longer flowing to the rest of my worthless body. The fact that my actions had led to the death of two innocent women was the worst thing that could have ever happened. My mind may have been fucked up, but I had never intended for good people to get killed because of their association with me.

Beverly and Laura were the only two who gave a damn about me when the rest of the world shitted on me. They supported me and didn't judge me, not even when I did shit that had them questioning my sanity. Once we became friends, they never turned their backs on me, not even when my mind led me to the darkened path I decided to walk down.

Now, more than anything, I wanted Aaron to kill me. Whatever he had planned for me, for however long he wanted it to last, I deserved it, every brutal moment.

Chapter Fourteen

Megan

At the first stop for fuel, I didn't lift my head to acknowledge Aaron when he asked me if I wanted to use the bathroom. When he climbed back into the truck and handed me a sandwich, I didn't reach for it. I remained slumped against the door, and my mind lingered in a tailspin that wouldn't stop.

Why the hell did Aaron even care if I ate or used the bathroom? He was taking me someplace to murder me. I was to blame for what he did to Laura and Beverly and for what he was about to do to me. It was my selfish actions that had led to this outcome. I would have to live with my friends' deaths for however long I had left. Hopefully, it wasn't long.

I hated Aaron for what he did. I wanted to see him suffer for killing my friends, but my fucking heart refused to let go of my feelings for him...feelings that I would stack into a pile on the ground and set afire if such a thing were possible.

Time passed in a blur as I sat and wallowed in my misery, not hearing or seeing the world around me. I hated myself more than Aaron ever could. I had no idea if hours or minutes were passing. I didn't care anymore.

When my bladder could no longer hold the large amount of water I'd drank after my evening run, I allowed my pee to flow out of me. Who cared if I was a piss-drenched mess? I got my friends killed, and I was about to be tortured and killed. I simply sat there in a catatonic state until Aaron picked up the scent of my urine.

"Megan, what the fuck!"

Aaron slammed his foot on the brake, making the tires squeal as they trembled under the weight of the truck. The sudden emergence of momentum lurched me forward. I didn't bother resisting the force of the impact and I would have likely hit the windshield if I hadn't been snatched back by the seat belt.

Due to the dark sky, Aaron tapped the button for the interior light, flicking it on. He glanced between my legs first before his gaze followed the wet trail that led to his floor.

"Goddammit, Megan! What the fuck is wrong with you? Why did you do that?"

I didn't answer, didn't even acknowledge that he was talking to me. I heard him, but at the same time, I didn't. I was in a vacuum; my mental focus was being sucked into a black hole.

Aaron gripped my shoulder and shook me, but I sat there and let myself get jerked around.

"What the fuck is wrong with you?" he asked again as his head pivoted between my face and the pool of piss at my feet.

Aaron hopped out of the truck, leaving his door open as he jogged around to my side.

When he cracked open my door, my body slumped over and hung out of the opening. The seatbelt kept me from tumbling to the ground.

Aaron shoved me back into the truck by my shoulder. The sound of cars zooming by on the road through Aaron's left open door registered, but my mind failed me, and I couldn't concentrate on anything but imagining my friends dying at the hands of a man my fucking heart refused to let go of.

"You're fucking crazier than I imagined you were," he said through gritted teeth.

With a firm grip on my shoulder, he shook and questioned me to find out what was wrong with me. This was how I handled my grief the first time I was raped by my foster father when I was twelve. I stopped talking for a month. My mind had decided to come back when it was ready.

Aaron reached across me and unhooked my seatbelt before he lifted me from his truck. He struggled to stand me up, when I was unable to get my mind to tell my legs to support my teetering body. He reached down to prop me up against the side of the truck after I slid limply to the ground.

I was vaguely aware of what was happening, but my mind was so filled with images of Aaron killing my friends, I couldn't think straight long enough to function normally. He left me there and walked away.

Him rummaging through the back of his truck sounded. He came out with a roll of paper towels and cleaning spray. He fussed and cussed at me as he wiped his seat and floor.

"I don't have the time to deal with a crazy-ass woman. Look at this shit. This is going to stain my seats. Fuck!"

Rubbing hard enough to shake the truck, he mumbled and grumbled as he cleaned the seat and floor with angry swipes.

"I can't believe this shit. Out of all the shit I could be dealing with, I end up with the craziest bitch in the state of Florida."

Once he was satisfied with the seat cleaning, he withdrew a large green blanket from the storage box in the bed of his truck and spread it across the seat. He proceeded to stand me up and deadlift me into the truck before reaching across me and securing my seatbelt again.

I was no help to him. My limp body slumped right back over to the open door. Aaron gave me a shove before he closed the door to keep from slamming me in it.

He hopped back in the truck and took off. His revving engine and sharp turns helped to translate his level of anger. It felt like minutes had passed when the truck decelerated to a crawl. The crunch of gravel and the unmistakable ditch-deep potholes in the road kept sneaking into the whirling chaos in my head before Aaron came to a stop.

We were at Aaron's house. Was he going to bathe me in acid and bury me with Chuck, Dutch, and Clint, the three men we killed inside his kitchen? It didn't matter. I deserved it. Out of all the crazy messes I made in my life, this one was unforgivable.

I chose the August Knights Motorcycle Club because nothing about any of them was innocent, so if something

I did led to their deaths, I wouldn't have cared. However, I would have cared about Aaron until *now*. Now, even he was on my shit list after what he did to my friends.

Chapter Fifteen

Aaron

I had to physically strip Megan, stand her in the shower, and bath her. She was stuck in a crazy-person, mute mode and was freaking me the fuck out. I didn't know how to deal with crazy people. Had I known she was truly insane, I'd have left her alone.

"Megan!" I yelled as I shook her, attempting to snap her out of whatever was wrong with her. "Shit!" I didn't know if I still wanted to kill her since she was obviously mentally ill.

She wasn't acting either. The light in her eyes had dwindled down to barely a flicker. She didn't look like the beautiful woman I knew. Her face was so devoid of emotion, it looked like a dark creature had sucked her soul right out of her.

I put her in my bedroom. After placing her in bed, I locked her in and went down to warm her a can of soup. A short while later, I attempted to feed her, but she wouldn't eat. She hadn't eaten or drank anything since I yanked her out of her apartment. Why was she like this? What was wrong with her?

She didn't acknowledge my presence either, not even when I threatened to kill her again. After forcing her to at least drink water, I made her sit on the toilet and pee before I tucked her into my bed and covered her.

Other than sitting on the bed next to her and watching her like a hawk, I didn't know what else to do.

She eventually fell asleep but tossed, turned, and yelled most of the night. She pleaded for someone to stop hurting her, and when she wasn't pleading for herself, she pleaded for others. She'd always slept restlessly, even talked in her sleep occasionally, but it had never been this bad.

The threats I made on her life must have triggered something. The longer I was around her like this, the less I wanted to kill her and the more empathy crept into my heart. Now, all I wanted to do was figure out what was wrong with her.

The next morning, she rose up out of the bed, an empty vessel on autopilot. I sat at the foot of the bed and watched her shuffle to the bathroom.

She bumped into the dresser like she didn't know it was there until she hit it. Her vacant eyes never focused on any specific thing. Her mind had traveled to another place, and I didn't know shit about how to get her back in the right frame of mind.

***

A few flickers of life eased back into Megan over the next few days. Although her expression remained empty, she at least swallowed her food and drank water when I gave it to her.

Afraid to leave her alone, I called off from work and extended my leave. Talking to Megan didn't work because her mind had vacated the premises, and only a shell of her remained. With my threat of killing her hanging over her head, she didn't even try to escape. Unless I physically got her up, she remained in bed, crying and staring at the walls with the covers up to her chin.

When I could no longer take the silence of the state she was in, I walked her down to the kitchen and sat her across the table from me.

"Megan, I'm not going to kill you. I never intended to. I need you to tell me how to help you. What's wrong? Are you like this because I threatened to kill you?"

Nothing.

"Does it have something to do with your childhood in Texas?"

Nothing.

I knew from studying her past that Megan's foster father and his nephew, her foster brother, had molested her, but I didn't want to remind her of it since it was likely what had caused her to be this way.

Maybe her brutally stabbing them was haunting her. Was I going to have to call Dr. Henderson? The doctor was our local fix-it man. He wasn't a head doctor, but maybe he could give me advice on how to help Megan.

For what seemed like hours, I sat across from her struggling to figure out what could have plunged her into this state. A random, yet rational idea struck me. She hadn't become this way until after I told her that I killed her friends.

I threatened to kill her, and she'd said nothing. I threatened to torture her, and she'd said nothing. But, when I told her that I killed her friends, she cried. She cried hard and hysterically. Was this her way of handling her guilt over her friends?

"Is this about your friends, Beverly and Laura?"

She glanced at me then with more life in her eyes than I'd seen since she pissed in my truck.

"I didn't kill your friends, Megan. I only told you that stupid shit to make you feel as bad as I did. I might be an asshole, but I'm not a complete homicidal maniac. If I'd known that something I could say could make you snap, I'd have kept my mouth shut."

A few more hints of life sparked into her teary eyes, enough to put a tint of color back in her ashen cheeks. After walking around the table to her, I made her stand before I took her seat and sat her across my lap. I snuggled her tight against my chest before wrapping her in my arms. She was as crazy as fuck, but I loved her.

Words I never intended to say to her bubbled to the surface and spilled over my vocal cords. The truest words I ever said to anyone sneaked past my lips and brushed over her earlobe.

"I love you, Megan. That's why I couldn't kill you. That's why I can't kill you. That's why I was so hurt when I found out you played my entire MC and me. And if that wasn't enough, you fucked my father, and I still don't hate you enough to hurt you. I still fucking love you."

At those words, her arms folded tighter around my neck as her body shook against mine. Her tears dripped down my neck as she repeatedly sobbed. "I'm sorry, Aaron. I never meant to hurt you."

Maybe Megan was playing me again. Maybe she was the ultimate manipulator that had enough practice to get what she wanted from anyone. Maybe she'd turned me into a big fucking fool-hearted idiot. I didn't know what to believe, what to think, or what to trust about Megan.

All I knew was that I loved the damn woman, and I couldn't overcome it. I couldn't turn the shit off. I couldn't beat it. She had a fucking hold on me that I couldn't fight. My heart was so twisted over her that I'm sure it was sitting sideways in my chest.

Megan slept snuggled against me. I held her while she fought whatever demons were haunting her. As impossible as it was to believe, I didn't bother her for sex. I wanted her to get better before I fucked the shit out of her again.

While lying there, I asked her to tell me what had happened in Texas. She nodded, acknowledging my request, but didn't say anything. I figured she would tell me the story in her own time, so I didn't press her.

***

The next morning, I found my bed empty and panicked, hoping Megan hadn't run away again. I ran out of my room, throwing a T-shirt over my head as I dashed down the stairs.

The sight of Megan standing at my stove, cooking, stopped me in my tracks. She offered a sad smile while leveling those big, brown, heart-tugging eyes on me. She was fighting her way back to normal or at least what she considered normal.

When she sat a plate of piping hot eggs, bacon, potatoes, and two fluffy biscuits in front of me, nothing could have taken the smile from my face.

"Thank you."

"You're welcome," she replied as she headed toward the refrigerator and poured me a big glass of orange juice.

She fixed herself a smaller portion of what she piled onto my plate. A smile teased my lips at the sight of her eating again. She nibbled at the food like a cute little wounded bunny.

My eyes followed the movement of her hand when she cleared her throat and reached across the table for my hand. Heavy emotions weighed her down as she struggled to tell me what was on her mind.

"I never meant to hurt you, Aaron. I hope you believe that."

I nodded. As much as I wanted to paddle her for what she'd done, I did believe she never meant to hurt me.

"I think I'm ready to tell you why I'm like this, why I'm so *broken*."

At those words, my brows lifted, and my interest level shot through the roof, but it wasn't going to stop me from finishing my plate of food.

Chapter Sixteen

Aaron

Although her head was downturned, it failed to hide the twinge of uncertainty coursing through the tense set of Megan's body. She was struggling to gather herself enough to tell me about her past.

When she lifted her head to meet my gaze, she couldn't hide the deep well of pain that lingered in her eyes and snatched at her rigid body. She released my hand and gripped her own. Her right hand gripped her left hand tight enough that the dark green veins pushed at the skin of the back of her hand and strained to break through.

"My caseworker placed me into the home of Carlos and Marina Dominquez. Carlos' nephew, David, lived there as well. I lived there for a month before my own personal hell broke loose. They seemed like nice enough people. They didn't beat on me and told me they liked that I was quiet and not a troublemaking a pre-teen. I was twelve going on twenty in street age and in life. I knew how to cook for myself. I had no trouble getting myself up and to and from school. I knew who I should and shouldn't hang out with. As a product of the foster care system, I witnessed all manner of crime and violence. I learned how to stay invisible and out of the way, but more importantly, I learned how to gather information, how to plan, and analyze."

A crease lined my forehead as I listened to Megan start her story. The foster parents' last name was ringing a bell, but I quieted my mind and continued to listen.

"I'd just started to settle in and assumed that every-thing would be okay when my foster father walked into my room one night and climbed into bed with me. Before I could get away, he pulled me against him. I fought him. I yelled, kicked, and screamed for help, but my foster mother and brother never came."

Her head fell to her chest as she wrung her hands. The memories were difficult for her to discuss. She inched her words out robotically, like saying them normally might be too much. Like if her emotions merged with the words she spoke, it would break a dam that had taken years for her to build.

"The more I fought, the more Carlos liked it. He laughed through my struggles and took my innocence like it was nothing. When I finally got around to pulling my-self from under the covers, I grabbed whatever clothes I could and ran out of that house with hair all over my head, crooked clothes, and no shoes. I looked every bit as crazy as people likely assumed I was."

No wonder she was all messed up in the head. I wanted to comfort Megan, but she needed to get this story off her chest more than she needed my comfort or pity, so I sat and listened.

"My foster parents called the police after I'd been out and on the streets for three days. I didn't care how I lived. I had no intention of ever returning to that house. But they told the cops that I was an out-of-control pre-teen who had run away because they refused to let me out of the house to go and see my nineteen-year-old boyfriend. It was all a lie they fabricated to take suspicion off my foster father and paint me as the bad girl. When the cops found me, I couldn't even speak up for myself to tell them what happened to me."

Megan cleared her throat and closed her eyes for a silent moment. Her past was what was haunting her, to the point of her losing track of her mind.

"When the cops dragged me back into that house kicking and screaming, they asked my foster parents to explain the bruises all over me."

Megan's dreary eyes lifted and stared into mine once more. The depth of her grief left me uncharacteristically speechless.

"They knew how to lie well. They claimed I bruised myself and threatened them with the idea that I'd pin it on them if they told the cops what I was up to. It should have been clear to the cops that I was in shock, but people see what they want to see. For all the lies my foster parents told, I never said a word to defend myself because I couldn't talk anymore, no matter how hard I forced my voice to come out. Even if I could, I don't believe it wouldn't have done any good. I was suffering mentally over being raped. My mind wouldn't or couldn't think past it. It seemed the only way to keep my anger at my foster parents from consuming me, was to stay quiet. I became obsessed with the idea of killing them. Knowing that my foster mom knew what was happening and freely helped a rapist, made me want to hurt her as badly as I dreamed of hurting my foster father."

Megan took a sip of juice and picked at her eggs. My plate was empty. I was about to tell her she didn't have to finish the story until she was ready, but she started up again.

"After weeks of silence and me not eating, I was not only an abused child, I started to look like one. A thinning body, dark circles around my eyes, and disheveled clothing, I went through the motions of going to school and back home. There wasn't a lock on my bedroom door, so I couldn't lock myself inside. The days and nights went by in a blur, and fifteen days after my first attack, my foster father returned. He took what he wanted, and again, I fought desperately, but he was too big, and my fight was useless. I remained in my silent state, and although I went to school, I stopped paying attention in class and doing my homework. Nothing outside of what was stuck in my head interested me. All I could think about was him raping me and me killing him for it."

I couldn't help myself. I couldn't sit there and watch Megan struggle through what was undoubtedly the worst thing that had ever happened to her. Reading about what happened to her and listening to someone else tell it secondhand was not the same as getting the story straight from the victim's mouth. The emotions and omitted details made what I once believed was a horrible story, real.

I didn't know how close Megan was to the end of her story, but what she shared so far, had anger raging through my bones and igniting my body.

I reached for her hand and couldn't help asking, "So this fucking foster mom knew what was happening and didn't do a damn thing?"

"As loud as I screamed, the neighbors should have known what was happening to me. The third time it happened, David, my sixteen-year-old foster brother, cracked and peeked into my bedroom door. I guess he wanted to see what he'd been ignoring. I wasn't sure if Carlos noticed him peeking, but I saw him and even pleaded for him to help me. David left me there after seeing what was happening to me. Three nights later it wasn't my foster father, Carlos, who crept into my room and climbed on top of me."

My head fell into my free hand as I squeezed my throbbing temples. I hated every part of the fucking story Megan was telling me. I bit into my bottom lip, but it did nothing to stave off my building rage. The inside of hell had been poured all over her young life, and she didn't have anyone to turn to for help.

"After about the tenth time, I stopped fighting them, but internally, I was keeping count. I kept count of how many times they raped me. The silence and my tears helped get me through it. Locking my pain in seemed like the only way to keep my mind and body from ripping apart. I dreamed about killing myself a lot. Laura and Beverly were the only girls who would talk to me at school. They would do silly stuff to get me to laugh. They were the only two people in the world who could temporarily take my mind off what was happening to me. It wasn't hard to figure out that they pitied me. I didn't have to tell them the details of what was happening to me. They were smart enough to figure it out or at least guess."

At this point, I didn't know if Megan wanted my comfort or not, but I continued to grip her hand. Megan was like a fucking puzzle to figure out, a jigsaw with parts that never stopped moving. I was learning her slowly, but I was learning.

There was more there than she was telling me about Beverly and Laura, I sensed it. The way she broke down when she believed I killed them was a story all by itself.

You don't break down like that just over friends. I was willing to bet that Megan was more connected to them than she was letting on. But I needed to be patient with her because her fragile mind was likely one crack away from shattering.

After a deep, steadying breath, she continued the story but kept her eyes aimed at the table.

"The abuse went on for months, but I found that the sexual abuse was only the beginning. Carlos was a monster. He started taking me out on weekend drives and forced me to lure other girls into the car with us. The first few times he asked me to do it, I was brave and denied his request. But denying Carlos only made the situation worse. He beat me so badly and forced me into sex so rough that I ended up in the hospital for a week. A broken wrist and bruises all over me and nobody, hospital staff or others who saw me considered getting me help."

She raised her arm and pointed out the scar on the inside of her left wrist. The huge gash I assumed was the result of a suicide attempt was instead the result of her being raped and beaten.

I glared at the jagged line of the scar with a pinched brow until she dropped her wrist. My hand slid over hers until my thumb skimmed lightly over the puckered line of the scar.

"The hospital didn't even do a rape test. Until this day, I have no idea what kind of story my foster parents fed the police or the hospital, but they fixed it so that no one was willing to listen to my side of the story or even concern themselves with asking."

My grip tightened around Megan's hand as I drew her closer. This shit she was sharing had me wanting to kill motherfuckers that were already dead.

"Come here," I said as I urged her closer to me.

She shuffled around the table before I directed her to sit on my lap. I tucked her into my arms and hugged her, rocking with her in my tight embrace as I buried my face in her neck. Her story helped me fully understand why her mind was twisted up like a knotted rope.

When I loosened my grip on her, she rested her head on my shoulder, and her words bounced off my neck. "He raped four girls in a two-year timeframe, and I'd helped lure them into his car. I sat in the front and listened to him have sex with those screaming girls in the back seat. Hearing them scream, beg, and plead for him to stop tore me apart worse than him raping me ever did. He wanted them young, like me—eleven, twelve, and thirteen-year-olds."

Her trembling arms squeezed tighter around me as she took in a heavy and shaky breath. She attempted to talk, but she became so overcome with grief, her words remained lodged in her throat. Hearing Megan's weeping cry fractured the strength of my resolve, and I closed my eyes to contain the sting in them. I'd never experienced this level of empathy before. Megan was dragging emotions out of me that made me realize that I was still human. It also made me realize how deeply I cared for her.

My hand swept up and down her back, aiming to ease the pain of what she'd endured. I didn't know what to say to her. There was nothing I could do to take this horrible shit out of her head. There was nothing I could do to make her not have those horrible fucking experiences. I couldn't do shit but hold her and pray she would one day win the battle over her pain. It was a pain etched so deep; it had soaked into her bones.

She forced words through her sobs, but I could hardly understand her.

"Megan, I didn't fully understand what you said, but it sounded like you said he killed those girls."

She sniffed and wiped her eyes, but no matter how much she wiped them away, the tears continued to flow. Her hands trembled so hard when I took them between mine, the movement shook my entire body.

Her bottom lip quivered as she fought to maintain control over her upset nerves. My throat tightened. Hearing and imagining the amount of pain she endured and seeing the amount of hurt still coursing through her body had my fucking nerves raw.

She shut her eyes tightly as tears seeped out and fell, leaving a trail down her cheeks. She kept going, forcing her words out.

"He killed them, and he made me watch. He raped them with me in the car listening. Afterwards, he would march me into the woods with them. He made me watch him while he killed them. He told me it was what he'd do to me if I told anyone or didn't do what he asked me to do. The suffering they endured at his hands was the scariest thing I had ever seen. He strangled one girl to death and got off on it. He came on her while he was strangling her. She screamed and hollered for me to help her, but I was too scared. All I could do was watch, cry, and scream right along with her. He strangled the next two and stabbed the fourth when it took too long for him to strangle the life out of her."

I was so filled with rage, hearing Megan's story that I took deep breaths to calm myself. "God, Megan, baby." I blew out a long harsh breath. I struggled with the images of what she went through. None of what she was telling me was in those news articles. This was the part of her horror that she'd likely not told another living soul. This was the part that had fractured her mind. This was why she was able to endure being around my MC. She had already experienced hell on every level. She'd felt it, smelled it, tasted it, heard it, and seen it.

"I'm so sorry you had to go through shit like that." I leaned my forehead down until it kissed the side of her head and rested against her curls. "Fuck," I growled as I clenched my fist.

After another deep breath that I blew out on a long exhale, I was ready to speak again.

"I'm glad you killed that motherfucker, Megan. I'm touched by darkness, but anyone who preys on innocent girls deserves their own room in hell. I promise you if he weren't already dead, I'd hunt that dead-dick bastard down and kill him myself. I'd kill him slowly."

A small smile curled Megan's lips after I revealed to her that I would kill Carlos if he was still alive. Pain drifted from her eyes as well.

"Over a two-year period, I was raped by Carlos and David while my foster mother did nothing to help. I lured four other girls straight into the hands of a monster who raped them before killing them. I may as well have been killing them myself. I couldn't take it anymore. If it had been only me, I probably wouldn't have killed my foster parents, but I couldn't let another innocent girl die."

Megan shook her head, seemingly shaking away the bad memories as she swiped at the tears leaking from her swollen, red eyes. This was why she wasn't bothered by witnessing death, especially the death of a man.

"I couldn't allow another girl to be raped and killed. Laura and Beverly came up with different scenarios on how I should go about handling my situation. Like lacing their drinks with antifreeze or cutting the brakes on the vehicle. I assumed that they meant their suggestions as jokes, teen girls talking about things they would never really do. But it was *Beverly* who had shoplifted the switchblade I used to stab my foster family to death with. She gave it to me to protect myself with. She told me her father, before he passed away, had made her carry one and taught her how to use it. She taught me where to stab a man in his inner thigh that would end him. I'm sure she had no idea I'd been daydreaming for months about ways I wanted to kill my foster family."

This explained Megan's loyalty to those women. They had attempted to help her and listened to her when no one else would. They had given her a weapon to protect herself against monsters.

"Two weeks after Beverly gave me the blade, Carlos came into my room. Marina and David were used to my screams, so I knew that they wouldn't bother to check out what was truly happening between Carlos and me. I waited until he took his dick out. The knife was in my hand the entire time. When he climbed on top of me, I jammed that blade in his neck with all my might. At the library, I had studied the different places to stab someone and what type of damage the wound would cause the body. While other teen girls were chasing boys and shopping for party dresses, I was studying effective ways to kill someone. I also made a habit of stopping at the various crime scenes that were a dime a dozen in my neighborhood. Seeing gunshot wounds and stab wounds on the streets also gave me an idea of what would kill a person. My situation turned me into a freak, a teen who studied death more than I studied textbooks."

A deep breath gave her enough strength to continue as her body rose and fell against the tight grip I had on her.

"I must have hit the right artery on Carlos that night because blood squirted from his neck like I'd opened a faucet. He was in such shock that he bled all over me before he realized he was dying."

Megan's tears had stopped when she spoke of killing Carlos. *Good.*

"I kept stabbing him everywhere, not caring where the knife landed as long as it went into his body. I stabbed him until my hands became too slippery to keep going, but that didn't stop me. I wiped my hands on the parts of my bed covers that weren't covered with his blood before I climbed on top of him. I sat, staring down at him whimpering and gasping in pain. I enjoyed seeing him suffer. I didn't have any remorse for what I was doing to him."

Her warm breath kissed my cheek when she lifted her head from my shoulder and glanced into my eyes.

"I was more in my right frame of mind while I was killing Carlos than I felt every time he raped me. He had the nerve to apologize, but I kept stabbing him. Although he was likely long dead, I didn't stop stabbing him until I reached the number of times, he'd raped me."

Megan sucked in a deep breath after dropping her gaze from mine. She had no idea how glad I was to hear that that bastard had suffered.

"When I walked into David's room, I found him lying in his bed asleep. I climbed into bed with him and started stabbing him through the covers. I didn't say anything to him as I took his life. He screamed and yelled loud enough to wake the neighborhood. He fought for his life, hitting and scratching me, but I was so consumed with rage and anger that I didn't feel his licks. I expected Marina to at least check to see why David was screaming, but she never came. Once I was done with him, I turned the blade on her."

Megan glanced up and searched my face. I suppose to see if I was viewing her differently. I was sure all she glimpsed in my eyes was hate for the people who hurt her.

"After the police arrived, they found me covered from head to toe in blood and muttering to myself about how I wanted to keep killing them. The authorities must have automatically assumed I was crazy. They cuffed me and drove me to the Pinewood Mental Institution where I spent a month before they transferred me out of the state of Texas to Ravencrest in Arizona. I don't know how the authorities were able to process me without a hearing or a trial or the legal processes I expected, but they did. They sent me to one of the most secure mental institutions in the country, and I was glad for it."

Megan eyed me for a silent moment. My eyebrows rose as her story continued to claw its way into my brain. I shook my head, attempting to shake off the gripping tugs of sorrow the story evoked.

"That was some story. Jesus," I uttered. I stared into Megan's eyes. "I'm so glad you killed those motherfuckers. How the hell did the state place you in that house with a fucking rapist, serial killer, a teenage rapist, and a wife who condoned it all?"

Megan shrugged. "I don't know. I never heard much else about it other than the authorities questioning me a few times each month for nearly a year. They left me alone after they were unable to get me to talk."

"Fuck. That's one of the sickest, coldest, stories I believe I've ever heard," I expressed. My voice was thick with emotion. "I keep picturing you younger and smaller, going through all that hell. I'm sorry, Megan. There are people in this world who deserve punishment, but not you, and especially not innocent, young girls who had never done shit to anybody."

Curiosity had me ready to ask her if she knew anything about her real family's background, but I left the subject alone for now. D hadn't found any family ties to

Lacey Daniels. The space for the mother and father's names on her birth certificate was blacked out, and Megan had been labeled a ward of the state. From the looks of things, Megan didn't have a history outside of foster care, so I along with her friends were essentially her only family.

After carrying her into the living room, I sat on the couch before I folded her into my chest. She'd seen and experienced shit that had chills running up and down my spine for hours. That type of shit sank into a person so deep; you would never get it out and you would never outrun it. She saw and experienced enough to drive anyone crazy. Megan fooled a lot of people, and she'd fooled me once, but she wasn't going to do it again.

I believed her story. I believed every word of it. I saw the emotion force its way out of her body. I heard the pain and anguish in every syllable of her words, but my gut was telling me that there was more. I sensed it just as I sensed something off with her the moment I laid eyes on her.

She wasn't ready to tell it all. She was keeping some secrets to herself. Just as it had taken time and a death threat for Megan to tell me about her horrible past, she would need more time to tell me the rest of her story.

Chapter Seventeen

Aaron

I inhaled a plate of cheesy grits, eggs, fat sausages, and golden, buttery toast, only pausing long enough to thank Megan for making me breakfast. Since her breakdown, I've been watching her like a hawk. My watchful eye grew even keener after she told me her story yesterday. She came back to me, but not all of her had returned.

Megan was the hardest puzzle I've ever tried to solve. Initially, I believed I knew enough about her to see a clear image come into focus. However, I think that there were more pieces to this woman that I couldn't see and that she wasn't revealing. I was certain that she had only revealed to me what she wanted me to know, making it difficult to help her. How was I supposed to help her heal when I didn't have a clue as to what she needed?

"I'm going to get you out of this house today," I blurted out. "I'll take you on a bike ride." My statement coaxed a fake smile from her as she sat in front of me picking at her food. She had gotten better, but she was no-where near back to normal…the normal I believed I knew.

One of her brows lifted at my statement, but she didn't say anything. I knew that look. Her mind had latched onto something she couldn't shake or get out of her head. I wanted her to tell me what she was thinking. I wanted to know everything, no matter how embarrassing or crazy. I wasn't afraid to admit that I didn't have my shit completely together, but I was willing to help Megan if she would just let me.

"I really should be getting back to my condo," she said as she scooted her chair back and headed toward the sink with her plate. After she tossed the food, she hadn't eaten down the disposal, a loud grinding noise sounded as my suspicious eye remained on her back.

Her movement away from the table was swift, but not swift enough. Tears were pooling in the corners of her eyes, which was the reason she jumped up from the table. Megan wasn't hurting physically, but she was suffering mentally. Seeing her this way and not being able to help her was killing me.

She wiped at the already clean countertop, a clear indication that something was bothering her. With clearer eyes, she glanced back at me. "I need to move my belongings. My lease will expire in a week."

This was her second time mentioning going back to her condo to finish packing. I was so upset with her when I was spying on her that I noticed but had chosen to ignore that she had already started packing. I recalled seeing boxes stacked in her bedroom and in the living room. She mentioned that she was packing and heading for South Carolina, but I didn't believe her for a minute.

I wanted to pull more information out of Megan, but I had to consider her fragile state of mind. Therefore, I treaded lightly and refrained from applying too much pressure by interrogating her. She didn't want me to know where she was moving to, and I was beginning to think she had a good reason why.

Why did I care? She wasn't my woman, and her problems weren't my concern.

Fuck.

Why was I lying to myself? I was obviously becoming obsessed with the woman.

"You need a few more days to relax," I suggested. Truth was I wasn't ready to let her go. "I'll go with you and help you pack if you think you'll run out of time."

She dropped her gaze and proceeded to clear my empty plate and glass from the table without answering me. I squinted, eyeing her suspiciously. She was hiding shit I intended to find out.

I still didn't understand why she concocted that elaborate plan to infiltrate my MC. She claimed it was a form of self-prescribed therapy; flirting with danger to understand herself better. It was a load of bullshit.

I flirted with danger damn near every day of my life and it did nothing in the way of helping me understand myself better. I believed Megan knew exactly who she was, but she was afraid to reveal herself fully to me for a reason I had yet to understand.

She'd revealed to me another chapter in her twisted life when she told me about her foster family, but she had many other skeletons buried deep inside her mind. How many more secrets was she hiding? Had she gotten herself into more trouble that she didn't see a way out of?

She wasn't wanted by the authorities as far as I knew and as far as D's digital reach went. Other than her frozen juvenile records, her life after Ravencrest as Lacey

Daniels had been as clean as a whistle. The thing that concerned me was the life she led under the different aliases she used.

What had Megan Jones, the writer, been up to? What had Kelli Hunter, another of her aliases, been up to? How many other people had she become? Why did it seem like she was running from something? Or better yet, why did it feel like she knew what she was running from? These were the kinds of questions I wanted answers to but was forced to keep to myself for now.

"Aaron, I know you don't care, but biking with me can be dangerous. Do you think it's a good idea to be seen around here with me on your bike? Despite your cousin's *ways*, I think Jake was right about the people around here not taking too kindly to us mixing, especially in a romantic way."

I flashed a smile at her. She wasn't going to talk her way out of this. This was something I believed might help her, and I at least wanted the chance to try it before she shot it down.

"I considered that," I finally told her. "I know a place we can go. I'll hitch the trailer to my truck, load the motorcycle, and we'll take a nice long relaxing ride."

A small smile crept across her mouth before she nodded and proceeded to wash the rest of the dishes. I sat watching, observing, eager to ask, but holding back the questions that had my tongue itching. Megan needed to heal more than I needed to satisfy my urge to figure her out.

Chapter Eighteen

Megan

The question of whether Aaron cared for me or not was answered. After what I pulled with him and his MC, he should have killed me, but he didn't. Said he couldn't. He had several opportunities to put a bullet in my brain, but he held back and stopped himself from doing to me what he would have easily done to someone else.

Although it was his fault for lying about killing my friends, he took care of me when I checked out on reality. However, there was one question that lingered in the back of my mind. Would Aaron have killed me if he hadn't inadvertently sent my mind into a frozen frenzy?

If he hadn't witnessed my breakdown, would I still be alive? I would like to believe so. I also believed that Aaron and I were of like minds; unpredictable, complicated, and twisted in a way that we may never be fully understood.

I was in such a distressed state when I believed he killed Beverly and Laura that my mind had gone into the black, retreating to that place that I prayed would save me from the heartache and pain. Instead, I allowed myself to cave so far into my despair that I couldn't figure out how to release myself from it.

This episode marked the second time in my life that I had fallen into this unchartered state where the darkness devoured me and left me helpless. My rape and the news of my friends' deaths was an overpowering blast that jolted my mental stability and sent me plunging into an endless well of unrelenting heartache.

What did it mean that I hadn't retreated into this dark place when my husband died? It didn't mean that I didn't love him. He was one of the people I would have done anything for. Maybe I was relieved that I hadn't been the reason for his death.

In the case of Carlos, I mentally reached into my deepest darkest corners and all I dreamed about was the many ways I wanted to kill and torture him. In the case of Beverly and Laura, all I saw was the endless ways Aaron, the man I believe I had fallen for, had brutally murdered them. I didn't understand why I reacted to situations in the way that I did, so I couldn't explain myself to Aaron or anyone else for that matter.

It was only when Aaron revealed that he hadn't harmed my friends that I found my way out of my own mind. Aaron had no idea that he'd saved me from myself by figuring out what had triggered me. He had metaphysically thrown a rope into the darkness and dragged me back to the right frame of mind. Or maybe my mind had released me. I didn't understand it and doubted the doctors that claimed to know the human mind could understand it either.

We had slept in the same bed together for the past five nights and hadn't had sex. Aaron hadn't bothered me for it since my breakdown, which was proof that he cared enough to hold back when I knew he wanted it. I wanted it too, but my mind wouldn't allow me the freedom I needed to go there with him.

My lips twitched at the images of the epic sex scenes we'd created together. If Aaron wanted it, mind still gone or not, he could get it.

I glanced out the kitchen window while standing over the sink. Leaves danced against an easy breeze as the clouds hung low in the sky insinuating rain. If there was one thing I learned about Florida, the weather couldn't be predicted off looks alone.

Aaron wanted to get me out of the house. Maybe getting out would do me some good since my brain kept crawling back to the darkness that clung to my mind and tugged at my soul.

***

Aaron drove in silence and although I stared out the window, I sensed his eyes on me. He was still on guard, being attentive to me and careful about what he said. The curious glint in his eyes and his stares, when he assumed I wasn't looking, told me he wanted to know more about my past and about why I sought out his MC.

He had a right to know the answers to his questions, but I wasn't sure how much of my past I should share with him. There was so much I hadn't told him about yet. Truth was, I don't believe I knew how to tell him certain things. Explaining them would be like untangling a pile of wires that had been twisting around each for years. There were also things I could never tell him.

142 · KETA KENDRIC

His hand landed softly atop my jean-covered thigh. I wore jeans and a tank under one of his long-sleeve black pull-over shirts. He was kind enough to help me into the shirt, which was large enough on me to be a jacket. Although the temperature was warm, I knew enough to know that the shirt would provide protection against road rash if things went bad during our ride.

"Not much further. Are you ready?" he asked me, squeezing my thigh.

I sat higher in the seat to take in our surroundings. "Yes," I answered, nodding. I was beginning to feel good about his suggestion of getting out of the house.

Occasionally, I caught stunning glimpses and scenes of water peeking from between the branches of the tree-lined highway as we traveled closer to the coastline. The interstate signs periodically indicated that we were headed toward Pensacola Beach, so the beautiful ocean view coming into focus had to have been of the Gulf of Mexico.

I inched my window all the way down and leaned into the sun-kissed breeze. I couldn't imagine ever growing tired of the beach or any large body of water because they represented freedom to me. They were massive bodies, so open, so awe-inspiring, and no matter how much we invaded them, they would never be fully explored. Their goal was to supply us with an escape, a respite from our everyday stresses. The beach provided that for me.

The crunch of small rocks under the tires became more distinct once Aaron slowed his truck down and turned into what I assumed was a parking area. He pulled into a slot, parking along a strip of paved land that was built between the highway and the ocean and served as a parking station for visitors. A few feet away from the parking space was an iron railing that kept visitors from falling over a steep one-story drop onto the bed of the sandy beach below.

I was up and out of the truck before Aaron. Anticipation and excitement coursed through me, filling in the dark spaces that fought to take over my mind. My tennis shoes scraped the paved ground as I made my way around the front of the truck toward the railing to get a better view of the peaceful scene that surrounded us.

Directly in front of me was the warm, welcoming ocean dancing against the skyline. To the left was an endless patch of trees that stood parallel to the ocean but far enough away that it left an opening for a sandy-topped haven that beach goers trekked across.

There weren't any trees to the right of us, which provided a wider area for vacationers and people to enjoy the beach. Some sunbathed, while others relaxed on towels, chairs, and under umbrellas.

It was hard to pick out distinct conversations, but the cheers of happiness and the excitement in people's voices couldn't be missed. Some swam and played water games, built sandcastles, and one group had a beach volleyball game going. Jet skiers could be seen further out in the water as they zoomed by, the hum of their engines revving as they enjoyed the high-powered excitement.

I leaned over the railing, relaxing automatically as I vaguely heard Aaron at the back of his truck unloading his motorcycle. He'd chosen to bring his Harley, saying he enjoyed it best for cruising the coast or for long drives. I didn't know anything about motorcycles, so I had no clue as to what was best.

Reluctantly, I stepped away from the view that continued to call me and approached the back of the truck. Aaron had already taken the huge motorcycle down and collapsed what I believed was a portable metal ramp. Red and black with shiny silver pipes running all over the place, the motorcycle was a beautiful piece of machinery.

Aaron closed and secured his truck as I continued to admire the bike. At an angle, I saw flames in the shiny red paint as well as in certain areas of the black paint. I was beginning to understand why some men admired their motorcycles and bragged about how good they looked and sounded.

When I worked for Aaron's MC, it wasn't lost on me that some of the men treated their bikes better than they treated their women. I bent to a stooping position, taking in the pipes and other parts I didn't know by name.

For such a tall well-built man, Aaron had a light and stealthy stride. He could sneak up on his own shadow. When I rose to stand, he was standing next to me handing me one of the shiny black helmets. The helmet was made to cover only the top of my head with a strap that buckled under my chin.

"Thanks," I said as I took the helmet and glanced up at Aaron who was adjusting his own over his head. Once I set it in place, my helmet swallowed my head as I copied Aaron, fiddling with the strap.

Aaron beckoned me closer when he noticed the chinstrap giving me trouble. My gaze roamed his body as he adjusted my strap. He wore a black long-sleeve shirt like mine. His cut was displayed over the shirt.

The heavy-looking black leather vest bore his MC's patches with a distinct patch that labeled him, Enforcer. I watched his muscles bulge underneath the black shirt as he secured the helmet on my head.

"What are you smiling about?" he asked me. Based on the hint of care in his tone and the smile in his eyes he was glad about me regaining my sanity. I'd certainly lost a part of myself and was thankful he didn't give up on bringing me back. Although he would never admit it, my actions had scared him.

"Us," I finally answered, trying but failing to keep my smile from growing wider. I twisted my lip, contemplating a question I wanted to ask him.

"How the heck did this happen?" For the life of me, I couldn't figure us out. We had chemistry from the start, but I was learning that there was a whole lot more than just chemistry between Aaron and me.

He shrugged, "I don't know. Although it may be hard to imagine, I do believe in God. I believe He wanted us together."

It was the last thing I expected him to say, but considering who we were and how we had come together, *God* was the only force powerful enough to make Aaron and me happen.

His hands dropped away from my face and slid down my shoulders before he released me fully. He slung his leg over the motorcycle and lifted the kickstand with the toe of his boot before he gripped the handle bars and leaned the heavy machine to an upright position. He patted the seat behind him, welcoming me aboard.

After placing my hand inside his, I climbed over the seat and snuggled in close, wrapping my arms around his strong torso as my legs rested snug against the outside of his.

I rested my head against his back and tightened my grip, enjoying being wrapped around his sturdy frame. I didn't recognize how tight my grip on him was until he rose to start the engine and took me up with him.

The powerful machine thundered to life, its burly roar vibrating against our bodies, reminding us of its strength. As smoothly as if he and the bike shared a connection, we took off. My head shot up and twisted and turned, swiveling on my neck.

We cruised out of the parking lot. I was sure I resembled an owl the way I twisted my head back in an attempt to snatch glimpses of the roving scene around us.

Once we turned onto the main highway, we shot off like a rocket. My arms tightened around Aaron's body as the momentum sent me lurching back a notch. Once I got over the initial shock and uncertainty of being exposed on a rolling jet, I lifted my head and took in the rest of the world as it zoomed by us in flashes of vibrant colors.

The rush from the speed and the idea that we shared this excitement together was like salve to my bruised mind. Like the beach, this bike ride was also freedom. This was the side of life that made you happy you'd survived the worst parts. Glad you fought through the madness because the opposite end of the spectrum made the fight worthwhile.

Aaron had known what I needed. I inhaled deeply and exhaled with a relieving sigh, as the ocean-misted air swished past my face. Once I settled into the free-flowing sensation of being hurtled through space atop a motorized rocket, my mind eased, and I relaxed.

A rush of contentment settled in my vibrating belly, and I snuggled in, gripping Aaron with all the strength I had in my body. I'd never experienced anything like this before. The strong man in my arms, the powerful machine roaring under my body, the space around us, rushing by as we breathed it in. This was how it felt to truly be alive, living in a moment of true happiness. Aaron had given me this precious gift, one that I will remember, cherish, and recall when times get tough.

We traveled over rising slopes and falling valleys. The trees bowed and swayed until the ocean disappeared and gave way to a lush, hilly countryside. Each time we descended a steep hill, Aaron would speed up and make the bottom drop out of my stomach, and I enjoyed the rush, giggling like a giddy teen girl.

Chapter Nineteen

Aaron

Although the time zoomed by like minutes, we'd been traveling for hours. I pulled into a small-town gas station to refuel and to see if Megan needed a break. I was too busy enjoying the scenery and Megan's laughter to notice the name of the town which was posted on the big green and white sign I failed to read miles back.

Once I pulled in next to the gas pump and cut the engine, I took Megan's hand to help her down. I then lowered the kickstand and allowed the bike to stand on its own.

"Do you need to use the restroom or want anything out of the store?" I asked. She shook her head no and it pleased me to see that satisfied smile on her face. She was enjoying this ride more than I expected she might.

"Shit," I cursed under my breath when I discovered the damn card swipe didn't work. I pumped the gas and left Megan standing next to my bike as I walked into the station to make my payment. Megan stood with her helmet hanging off her fingers as she stared at the scenic country view.

After entering the station, I greeted the attendant with a quick head gesture. "Pump three."

The sound of loud rock music caught our attention and dragged my curious gaze to the opposite side of the pump to where Megan stood. A shiny black Mercedes had driven up and parked.

Once the vehicle stopped and the music died, the occupants' loud voices carried but their words were unclear.

"That will be fifteen," the attendant said, regaining enough of my attention for me to hand him my debit card.

I leaned over and peeked around the pump to get a better look at the black Mercedes. The passenger exited the vehicle to stretch his legs while the driver stepped around to pump the gas.

It wasn't hard to tell that they were privileged and used to getting whatever they wanted in life. They carried themselves in a way that insinuated that they believed they were better than everyone else. Their expensive, shiny car and designer clothes spoke volumes. They were too over-dressed for this small town and must have been heading to one of the larger cities.

The driver's face bore a deep frown when he discovered the card swipe didn't work. Megan stood facing my bike now with her back to the men. My gaze followed the driver's expensive leather shoes as he stepped around the pump and made his approach toward the entrance. His designer suit and perfect hair flapped in the wind. The man was polished down to his socks. His expensive watch flickered when the sun hit it just right. The douche bag probably hadn't put in an honest day of work in his entire life.

When he glanced back and caught sight of Megan, his steps halted, and he stood glancing over his shoulder at her. *Keep walking, motherfucker.* The bastard turned his polished ass toward Megan, intent on bothering her. She had his attention without even realizing it. A deep calming breath did nothing to remove the tension building inside me.

"Sir," the attendant called to get my attention.

I had no idea how long the man was calling me because I was too busy watching that asshole who was now talking to Megan. "Yes," I finally answered.

"Can you enter your pin, please?"

I entered my pin number and my attention immediately returned to Megan and the snobbish asshole who was standing way too fucking close to her.

It was obvious she wasn't listening to what he was saying, and my assumptions about him were turning out to be right. He was one of those arrogant pricks who didn't take no for an answer, especially where women were concerned. Once I entered my pin and retrieved my debit card, I headed for the door.

"Sir, don't you want your receipt?"

"No," I answered without looking back. When I opened the door, Megan's gaze met mine and she froze. Blazing red heat flashed across my vision when I saw a hand on her arm. The bastard was too busy eyeballing her to notice the Grim Reaper lurking at his back.

"If you want that fucking hand, I suggest you release her wrist." Acid may as well have been dripping off my lips. I sensed Megan's eyes on me as I was sure death flashed across my face.

I stood so close to the man, the tip of my boot brushed the front of one of his expensive shoes. The punkish bastard backed up a few paces and threw up the hand he'd been using to touch Megan. He cast a hard glare, his eyes wide and mouth agape.

"Sorry. I don't want any trouble," he said as his gaze raked over me from head to toe. Out of the corner of my eye, I could see his friend peeking around the pump at us.

The asshole in front of me was still standing too close to Megan for my liking, and he kept glancing from her to me. His thoughts were playing out all over his curious face as he had the audacity to turn his nose up at me. He was no doubt questioning if we were together.

"Is there a fucking reason you're still standing here?" I asked him, my face pinched into such a tight grimace, my top teeth grinded into the bottom. However, I was proud of my control because a seething mass of rage was dying to exit my body. The man didn't get a chance to answer me because his wanna-be-brave-ass friend stepped around the pump.

"Is there a problem here?" the friend asked, in a raised voice as he approached and stood next to the one who'd had the nerve to touch Megan. The sight of him with his hand on her had my fucking beast roaring to be set free. They must think that the two of them together could take me, but I was ready to fuck them up if they tried me.

The first step I took toward them was stopped by Megan. She stepped in front of me and wrapped her small hand around my clenched fist as her other hand dug into my waist.

"Let's go, Aaron," she said into my chest because my blazing gaze was still on the assholes standing in front of me who were growing more arrogant by the second. They might have been arrogant, but they knew enough not to test a snarling dog. I was ready to set their fucking world on fire if they moved an inch.

My hand skimmed up Megan's arm after I took the helmet from her hand with the other. I set it in place on her head and buckled the chin strap. One last glare was set on the two in front of me before I gripped the handlebar of my bike and climbed over it.

I put my back to those fucking dicks. I wanted them to try something because I needed an excuse to rip them apart. My fucking blood still boiled over one putting his hand on Megan.

I didn't have to look back to know that they were still standing there watching us. Megan took my hand and allowed me to help her onto the back of the bike. Her sexy-ass legs wrapping around me and her arms sliding around my chest eased my tension.

I kicked the bike to a roaring start and revved my engine before I shot off, leaving a huge gust of smoke and burnt rubber in those assholes' faces.

They didn't even deserve another glance from me. Besides, I was the one who had what they wanted. And if it hadn't been for Megan, they would have been swallowing their fucking teeth.

She snuggled against my back, tightening her hold around my body. A wide grin of satisfaction spread across my lips.

Cruising on my bike was one of the joys in my life. It took me out of my own head, eased my mind, and relaxed my body. It made me forget about the problems that living a life like mine guaranteed. It occurred to me before, but I believed Megan did the same thing for me. She offered me a peace of mind I couldn't get anywhere else.

Until we encountered those pricks at the gas station, our time together was perfect. Megan needed this whether she realized it or not. It had been months since I'd taken a ride on one of my bikes, so I needed this mind cleansing experience as much as she did.

Chapter Twenty

Megan

Aaron had been ready to rip those guys apart back there. I saw hell's fury flash in his eyes. The trust-fund kings had no idea how close they came to a hospital visit all because one had made the mistake of touching me. The man hadn't even given me a chance to say no to his proposal to take me out. His privileged arrogance had no doubt allowed him the freedom to say and do what he wanted.

Aaron was arrogant too. However, he had enough fire in his soul to back up his arrogance. I liked seeing him being possessive about me. The idea that he was willing to fight for me warmed my heart and had me clinging to him even tighter.

There hadn't been many people in my life that were willing to fight for me. The few I encountered meant everything to me, and I would sacrifice my life to save theirs. Beverly and Laura were two of those people. It was why I had taken their deaths so hard when I believed Aaron killed them.

When the swirling wind slowed, and the roar of the bike decreased to a gentle rumble, I glanced around Aaron's sturdy shoulder to see why we'd reduced speed. He turned the motorcycle onto a dirt road that opened to a small strip of private beach mostly overgrown with trees and grass.

Aaron stopped the bike at the edge of the dirt road before it softened into sand. He shut off the engine and assisted me off the bike before he climbed off. "Let's rest here for a while. Take in the scene."

My smile widened at the idea. "I'd love to. Thank you."

Aaron taking in a scene? I didn't say anything, but he wasn't the kind of man who would take in a scene. He was either letting me see a little more of his true self or doing this scene-taking expedition for my benefit. Either way, I appreciated the efforts he took to lift my spirits.

Another shot of contentment sprang up in me as we inched closer to the water's edge. My tennis shoes sank into the sandy surface, making me want my bare toes flirting with the sand.

We stood on the small sandy area that separated the tree line from the swaying water and stared out at the ocean. When tiny droplets of mist mixed with the breeze swept over our bodies, I threw my head back and let my eyes drift closed before taking in a deep breath. Aaron stood motionless, staring out into the ocean with his hands at his sides.

"Thank you for this, Aaron. I didn't know how much I needed this until you gave it to me."

I stepped in front of him, stood up on my toes, and feathered my lips over his stubbly cheek. He turned his face so that my lips fell into the grooves of his. My arms encircled his strong torso as I inhaled his refreshingly

masculine scent and relished the feel of his strong muscular body.

"I needed this too," he said before he placed a kiss on
my forehead. He drew me in tighter, enclosing me into his
strong hold with a throaty groan. His warm breath swept
through my hair and warmed my neck.

"I hated seeing you like that. I hate what you went
through. I hate not being able to do shit about any of it."

I could hear the concern in his voice. Seeing me that
broken and outside of myself had scared him. Hearing
about the past that had driven me to that point added another layer to the grief he harbored for me.

Aaron's face nuzzled deeper into my neck, and he inhaled me before releasing a deep sigh. I enjoyed being
wrapped so tightly in his arms. I felt safe, protected. The
way he held onto me, Aaron made me feel precious, like
I meant the world to him. Did he have any idea how he
made me feel?

I eased back, causing him to loosen his grip when I
glanced up at him. I had to have a kiss. Other than that
night in my condo, we hadn't shared any passion.

The kiss I initiated was short, sweet, but not enough.
I needed more. The look in Aaron's eyes said he wanted
more too. We went in for another kiss that left us breath-
less and seeking out body parts with frenzied hands. Lust
bubbled to my surface, seeping into the air like an exotic
perfume.

Had Aaron noticed? Yes, he had. I believed he knew
me better than anyone else. If that smile dancing in his
gaze was any indication, he saw my lust and was about to
turn it into a burning desire.

I went up on my toes again, and he leaned down until our lips collided. The urgency in our kiss was apparent. This was the fifth day that we'd been together and hadn't had sex. For me and Aaron, five days of abstinence while we were under the same roof was a miracle.

Briefly, I backed away to catch my breath, but I didn't stay for long. We dove right back in, clawing at each other, nipping and tugging.

My harsh breathing sent my words out in a rush. "Aaron, I'm ready."

I didn't have to explain myself to him. He glanced into my eyes and knew what I wanted.

"Okay, let's go because you've got my dick as hard as a damn steel support beam," he revealed as he gripped my hand and dragged me toward the motorcycle. I had to jog to keep up with his long, quick strides. When he climbed onto the bike and reached for my hand to help me, I took the hand he offered but didn't move to climb onto the bike.

Instead, I walked around his leg and stood facing him. "I didn't mean, ready when we get back. I meant, I'm ready *right now*."

If there was one thing I knew, Aaron would give me some sex, and I didn't think he cared much about where he gave it to me. He eyed me before his tongue slid between his lips.

He stood, leaving the bike straddled between his legs. It remained standing on the kickstand as he leaned over and gripped my waist. A deep gasp escaped when he lifted me onto the bike with him and seated me in front of him.

My legs ended up hiked up over his, my pelvis pointed upwards.

He didn't have to nudge me or instruct me further. I gripped the tail of his vest and inched myself closer, not stopping until the warmth of my core was snug against the hard bulge his jeans barely contained.

He leaned down and took my tongue as my arms went up and crossed behind his neck. My hot pussy danced against his hardness as my hips automatically took on a rotating motion.

"This shit ain't going to work," he said as he filled his hands with my tits, squeezing them through my shirt. It wasn't until the unsteady bike wobbled underneath us that I understood his statement. My eager movement and our heated passion were going to cause us to fall.

"Let me help you down," he whispered hotly before nipping my neck once more. "I have an idea."

He didn't have to tell me twice. He assisted me as I climbed off him and the bike. It didn't take him but a second to be at my side. He took a moment to adjust his dick before he took off and entered the trees, gripping my hand and dragging me behind him. I giggled, but understood the urgency in this situation.

The short hike took us into a cluster of trees but didn't completely hide us as I was still able to see parts of the motorcycle. Aaron found a small clearing lined with leaves and grass among the trees, the spot I prayed he was about to fuck me in.

He shrugged off his black leather vest and spread it across the grassy part of the ground. Part of the ocean was still visible from our location and we were close enough to the highway that I could hear cars passing although the trees blocked them from my view.

The sound of the ocean massaging the beach's edges was our music. Chirping birds and singing insects added to the natural harmony.

When Aaron flicked the button loose and snatched the zipper down on his jeans, I started tugging at my own jeans. An urgent pang of lust shot to my core when his dick popped out of his boxers. My eyes landed on the splendid piece and didn't move as I continued to take down my pants and panties.

I was so hypnotized by Aaron's dick that he walked up to me, gripped my shoulders, and nudged me down to the vest he laid out. He hadn't bothered with taking his shirt off and neither did I because the parts we needed most had been set free.

My bare ass kissed the inside lining of Aaron's vest, which was large enough to keep my back and ass off the grass. I didn't have to worry about my legs, they were going to end up around Aaron's back or over his shoulders. As hot as he had me, I didn't care where he put my legs as long as he was between them.

He kneeled in front of me and my legs fell apart. His gaze locked with mine, watching me as I sat up on my elbows watching him through hooded eyes. He inched closer and I spread my legs wider. If someone exploring this area walked along or drove down that small dirt road we drove on, they would end up spotting Aaron and me about to fuck, and I didn't care.

He placed one hand on my knee before letting the other slide down the inside of my thigh until his fingers splayed my lips and circled my clit. I gasped at the first erotic touch and my breath hitched when his thumb slid across and pressed against my nub.

"Good girl, you're already wet for me," he stated, his gaze as heavy with lust as mine.

When his fingers left my throbbing, wet core, he angled his body so that the swollen head of his dick kissed my clit. He inched closer so that the head pressed and slid up and down my clit, teasing it and sending hot sparks of pleasure racing up my back.

Leaning forward, his dick slid down one last time and kissed my sopping wet heat before nudging the opening. He didn't force his movements nor was he in a hurry to plunge into me. He eased his dick in with one long thrust that caused every muscle in my body to clench so tight I believed they might snap.

"Fuck!" fell from my mouth before my teeth sank deep into my bottom lip. My head fell back onto the grass as I sought any part of his body to hold. When he pushed as far as he could go, he gritted his teeth, forcing air between them before he eased back out and plunged forward. He repeated the action until he was all the way in, gasping as hard as I was heaving.

Once he had a good rhythm going, Aaron leaned down and covered me with his hot body. The weight shift increased the impact of his hard thrust and sent his dick probing deeper. I don't know how my legs ended up draped around his muscular back, but there they were riding the rhythm of his movements.

"You have no idea how much I missed this pussy," Aaron ground out. His hot words added fuel to my blazing lust as his warm breath floated over my face. A strong hand slid up my thigh, gripping it in a tight hold as his thrusts grew more urgent and forceful. My heavy breathing kicked up a notch, keeping pace with Aaron's dominating movements.

I had fallen so far into the pleasure Aaron powered into me, that I didn't notice the grip he had on my thigh was transferred to my ankle. He dragged my foot away from his back and with my ankle in his tight hold, he lifted my leg, opening me even wider. His attempt at repositioning me hadn't interrupted his lustful movements.

My leg continued upward until my inner thigh rested against his bicep, my foot flapping in the wind with each hard thrust he delivered. With his strong arm under the back of my knee, I wasn't going anywhere, not that I intended to anyway. When he reached down for the other leg, I assumed he would raise it as well, but his hand stopped at my hip and his fingers dug into my warm flesh.

"Fuck!" he growled before pounding harder, his flesh smacking against mine as his dick tunneled deep inside me, taking my breath away. When Aaron started dropping F-bombs, it meant he'd found the most intense pleasure zone, which always ended up being mutually beneficial.

"Shit. Aaron. Oh God. Fuck!" Between my *shits* and *fucks*, I was saying shit that didn't make any logical sense. I had no idea how long we'd been fucking, but he had me on the verge of blowing up and lighting those damn trees on fire.

I didn't care that we were outside and in broad daylight. I didn't care if someone walked onto the beach and saw us. I didn't care if someone could hear us screaming and vocalizing our pleasure.

Deep breaths hissed out of my mouth as I took his hard pounding, savoring the overpowering sensation of him driving his dick deep inside me. He forgot about the plan he had in mind for my other leg. One leg lay over his powerful arm and the other remained splayed at his side as I clawed his back and sucked on his tongue when he slid it into my open mouth.

I gasped for both air and at the fierce pounding I had no choice but to take. When my lips ended up near his ear, I couldn't help releasing a few hot words of my own.

"You said you missed this pussy, but I missed this dick more."

"Fuck, Megan. Shit. You're going to make me cum," he breathed out through gritted teeth as his fingers dug deeper into my hip in a bruising grip. I writhed under him as involuntary trembles quacked through me. The anticipation of my orgasm drove me so close to the edge, I was ready to jump. I held back as much as I was able to, not wanting this sinful goodness to end.

My desire to stretch this scene out was washed away by the haze of pleasure that swept over and through me until I fell over a cliff of shameless madness. I shattered as fragments of my mind clung to reality but lost the battle at keeping me sane.

Aaron was large enough that sparks of pain were always entwined with my pleasure. At this point, I believed the pain was a necessity and the pleasure couldn't exist without it. I enjoyed the intoxicating mixture coursing through me while Aaron stretched me to the point of him being one notch from breaking me.

He roared into my ear as he pulled me into his chest so tight, I could hardly breathe. He dropped my pinned leg and shoved his strong arms under my shoulders and tugged me down to meet his hard thrust. I was on the verge of passing out, but he shuttered and came so hard his body froze before his pounding thrusts returned to complete the mind-numbing experience.

We lay there for a minute, recovering and enjoying being connected to each other. The warmth and afterglow of our sex was the most relaxing experience in the world. When Aaron began to inch out of me, I stopped him. "Just a little bit longer. I love feeling you inside me."

The comment lit up his face, making him smile. When he shifted back into place, snuggling closer, I could feel his semi-hard dick tickle my walls. Still breathing heavily, our chests pounded against each other as we lay there in the moment, not talking but just breathing and allowing our warm breaths to float away into the wind.

Only when my legs started to ache from the position they had fallen into at his sides, did I loosen my grip on Aaron and allowed him to take his dick out of me and get up. He staggered up to a standing position and I sat and shamelessly watched him tuck his dick back into his boxers before he tugged his jeans up. Once he finished, he reached a hand down to assist in pulling me to my feet.

Since we didn't have anything to clean ourselves with, I slid my damp ass back into my panties and jeans, wobbling the entire time on sex-weakened legs. It wasn't until Aaron reached down for his vest that I saw that our juices had been smeared all over the inside of it.

Aaron raised the vest and took a glance at it before he threw it on over his long-sleeve shirt. It didn't matter, we were both soaked in each other's juices anyway.

We hiked back to his bike slower than we had hiked into the woods, but we were smiling, happy, and satisfied.

No words were exchanged between us on the ride back to Aaron's truck. We simply enjoyed the beautiful scenery laid out for us as we cruised.

Chapter Twenty-one

Aaron

A deep sigh left me as I watched my father fail to control his anger. He'd been ripping into me for minutes as I sat and watched him. I expected him to be upset, so I didn't disturb his outburst.

"Have you lost your fucking mind? You mean to tell me that bitch is at your house right fucking now? This can't happen. You can't carry on a fucking relationship or whatever the fuck you think you're having with her. One, she's black in case you've forgotten that. Two, she played all of us like fucking fiddles."

My father's evil-eye glare was almost comical, but I hid my amusement under a serious expression of my own. His heightened voice danced all over the boardroom. The roar of drunken bikers outside the door in the clubhouse swept in through the cracks and reminded me that there was a world outside those doors that could kill me for the few sentences I'd spoken to my father about Megan.

"Need I remind you for the hundredth time, we are a *white* MC that don't deal with *blacks* unless it's business? And even that's iffy. How do you think this shit is going to play out? The president's son, running around claiming a black woman?"

My sharp gaze met my father's across the club table, but I remained silent, allowing him to get his ranting and raving out of his system. The vein in his forehead protruded as he cursed. His roaring voice was loud enough to peel wood from the table, but I hardly understood a damn thing he was saying.

My mind was made up. Therefore, no amount of cursing or yelling on my father's part would sway my decision about Megan. The muffled voices outside the club made more sense than my father's red-faced, raging words did. The fact that I wasn't responding to his jaw-jacking eased some of the tension he was spilling into the room.

At least I waited until the rest of the MC's chairmen had exited the room before I approached my father about my situation. All my father knew was that Megan had made a fool out of all of us. He didn't know the full story, and I wasn't going to tell it to him because he wasn't going to care either way. So, I sat and watched him fail to comprehend my ability to forgive Megan.

Forgiveness wasn't a part of my father's genetic makeup. Hell, it wasn't a part of mine either, but when it came to Megan, nothing I did before, no rules or guidelines, not even her mental state was enough for me to walk away from her.

Therefore, there was no way I intended to listen to my father and *get rid* of her as he kept insisting. Even if she didn't have a horrible past, I wouldn't have hurt her anyway.

I had finally accepted what I was fighting all along. I not only cared about Megan, I *loved* her. Before now, I never understood the whole concept of love. To me, it was always about being a man and taking charge of your emotions. Only a fool would let something as intangible as a four-letter word rule their lives. I was learning a life lesson in a short amount of time, and like most lessons in my life, I chose to learn it the hard way.

Love was something you would never understand unless you experienced it or became possessed by it. It wasn't something you could shake off. It wasn't something you could fight or control. It wasn't something you could decide on because it decided on you. Once love had a hold of you, you became a slave to its power and you either embraced it or ended up spending your life running from it.

Initially, I ignored it. Then, I struggled to fight it. I even spent time attempting to destroy it. It wasn't until I embraced it that I found enough peace in it to move forward with my life. Sitting in front of my father was proof that there was nothing I wouldn't do for Megan.

When I could take no more, I met my father's irritated gaze with one of my own. He sat there acting like I was the crazy one when he had slept with Megan too. He would have slept with her again if she would have agreed to it and I allowed it.

He was the biggest judgmental hypocrite I've ever met. Many in the MC had allowed my father to sample their women just to stay on his good side or to get him to agree to the illegal shit they were into. Many of the men traded women for sport regardless of the reasoning.

"Shark, you know me," I finally said. When I called my father Shark, he knew I was stepping over the son title to embrace the title of MC chairman.

"You know I would not have hesitated to put a bullet in that woman's brain if I didn't have a good reason not to. I—"

"You've got a good reason all right. She put that pussy on you and got you whipped." Shark's frown deepened. "But you're going to have to shake that shit off, man the fuck up, kill her, and find you a good wholesome white girl to play house with."

He fucking cut me off. My brows pinched so tight; I could literally feel them bumping each other. My menacing glare was no doubt alive with the heat of my anger. I leaned over the table, inching closer to my father. I had a ton of respect for him and seldom back talked him. This wasn't one of those times. My voice erupted from my mouth low, sure, and clear.

"I don't give two fucks about what you think. I don't give two fucks about what this MC will say. If it wasn't for the illegal shit I do, the illegal deals that I broker in the name of this MC, there wouldn't be a fucking MC. We'd be a bunch of poor redneck assholes with missing teeth and beer bellies, hating on black people because we can't stand the fucking sight of our own damn faces. If it weren't for Megan, I'd be dead, so you can tell the other chairmen whatever the fuck you want. If I don't make the gun run in a month, none of you will have two copper cents to rub against each other."

My father gasped and jerked his head back, like my outburst was a hard smack across his angry face. I stood, slamming my legs back on the sturdy, wheeled black chair so hard, I almost toppled it. I could hear the chair stumbling and rolling behind me until it banged into the wall.

I stomped off toward the exit. My tight grip nearly ripped the rusted knob off the door. The door swung open so hard, the wind gusted past my face, and it slammed into the wall behind it. The loud crack of the door sounded over the music and chatter outside the room. The *boom* sent heads in the clubhouse turning in my direction. I was a big dude at six-feet-two, two hundred and ten pounds, so I was sure I looked like an angry giant about to barrel his way through the clubhouse.

"Son! Son! Do you think I'm going to stand by and let you ruin your life over some black bitch?"

My back stiffened at my father's angry words, but I didn't glance back at him. When I crossed the threshold out of the office and entered the club, Shane, my cousin and one of our chairmen, almost fell on top of Wade, my uncle, who was another of our chairmen.

They scattered out of my way like disturbed ants. Jake turned his back and pretended he was talking to a random person who wasn't paying him any attention. They couldn't properly hide that they'd been listening at the door. Their snitching eyes and animated body postures gave them away.

If they overheard any of my discussion with my father, they knew that I was claiming Megan. I couldn't say that she was my old lady, nor could I call her my property because she was more important to me than the titles we often assigned our women.

I had no intention of following the warped no-black rule my MC had half-heartedly scribed into our bylaws. If any of them threatened to throw the book at me, I fully intended to call out every rule that each one of those bastards was breaking. They didn't care about me breaking the rules to get them money, so they sure as shit shouldn't care about who I chose to spend my time with.

Since these leeches had likely overheard the news about Megan and me, it would spread like wildfire. I wasn't worried, though. All I had to do was raise my voice and most of them would scatter like roaches.

Seventy or maybe even eighty percent of the money the club made came from the guns that I was running. If they chose to vote me out, they were stupider than I assumed. My uncle, Charles, gambled most of the money from the strip clubs away, the bar barely broke even, and half of the MC, including a few of the chairmen, got high in some form or fashion, so drug profits were marginal at best.

No one uttered a word to me as I headed toward the front door. Not the three who'd been eavesdropping, nor the other members and prospects scattered throughout the clubhouse, eyeballing me with their lips hanging open.

My face was frowned in such a hostile glare that they stepped back out of my path so as not to frustrate me further. I sensed them all staring a hole in my back as I approached the front door. With my hand against the frame of the door, I paused right before I shoved it open.

When I turned back, those fucking cowards turned around so quickly, you'd think I had a remote controlling them. A wicked smile spread across my mouth before I walked out of the door and headed to my truck.

I was headed home to Megan after having told my father and the rest of my MC, as far as I was concerned, to fuck off. They were going to be upset about me being with her, but they were too chicken to approach me and tell me to my face. All they were going to do was whisper behind my back and drive my father crazy trying to convince him to talk what they assumed might be some sense into me.

As much as I'd like to, I wasn't going to flaunt Megan around them. She'd been through enough and although she didn't realize it, she was punishing herself worse than anyone else.

Megan had intentionally placed herself in dangerous situations sometimes, aware the result could end in her death. I was no head doctor, but I would venture to say that she hadn't forgiven herself for luring those girls to her foster father and watching helplessly as he raped and killed them.

Chapter Twenty-two

Aaron

The aroma of the delicious dish Megan was preparing greeted me when I strolled through my living room door. Nothing about the woman made sense. Looking at her, you didn't see a killer or a cook or even a sexy vixen. But she was all three and then some.

A tasty meal and all the good sex you could stand—what more does a man need?

When I stepped into the kitchen, Megan was standing over a pot, stirring something I knew would be delicious. Her purple earbuds blasted tunes into her ears. Her bare feet glided across the kitchen floor, and all she wore was one of my white wife beaters. When she bent over the sink to place something inside, the shirt crept up and flashed a set of purple panties draped over the nicest, firmest ass I've ever caressed.

I was at ease again, seeing her return to her old self after her mental shut down. I'd never seen anyone like that in my life.

After I crept up behind her, my eager lips floated over her warm neck and my hand slid around her slim waist. She leaned her head back against my chest, keeping the ear buds in. I could hear the vocal crooning of Sia buzzing in her ears.

My hand slinked down the T-shirt to fondle her curves. After lifting the tail end of the shirt, my hand slinked down into those cute little purple panties.

She never stopped me when I took what I wanted, so I was free to let my hand slide lower until my fingers parted her lips. "Fuck!" fell from my mouth at the realization that she was already wet.

I let my middle finger circle her clit a few times before dipping my finger into her wet opening. A cute whining whimper left her mouth before her body folded over my arm. I worked my finger in and out of her, making her slicker and slippery wet with every stroke.

With my big hand planted in the center of her back, I readjusted our positions and bent her over the sink. I couldn't wait until after dinner. I had to have some now. As far as I could recall, I'd ripped at least three pairs of her underwear. Since I liked the silky ones she wore now, I slipped them to the side after I freed my dick, which had been hard during my drive home because I was thinking about her.

With the music continuing to blast in her ears, I used my feet, shoving them against the inside of hers to spread her legs wider. Her body fell further over the sink as my hand slipped back into the front of her panties. When my dick was lined up just right with her warm, sopping wet entry, I plunged into her with one long, hard stroke that didn't stop until I couldn't go any further.

My finger circled her clit from the front while I thrusted slowly from the back. My grunts competed with the blare of the ear buds in her ear as my harsh breaths swept through the air and picked up strands of her fluffy curls.

Each deep breath I took swept up my nose and mouth, raced down my chest, and filled my lungs with the floral fragrance emanating from her hair and soft skin. My anxious fingers gripped her shoulder and tilted her back to ensure she was arched just right.

I drove my dick in harder while grinding the thrust once I was in all the way. My God, this woman had a treasure trove of pleasure hidden between her thighs. She had me so addicted to her sex that I became a fucking sex fiend for her, peeking around every corner looking for my next hit.

My father had been right about one thing; I was whipped, but not in the way he assumed. It was not just her pussy that had taken me prisoner, it was her—the whole package. Both my heads were gone, and I had reached the point of no return.

Eventually, I would have to let Megan get back to her life, but right now, I couldn't. I couldn't get enough. She wasn't stingy with the sex either. If I fucked her five, six, seven times in a day, she'd still be ready. Her sexual appetite was as ferocious as mine.

The ear buds continued to blast as long moans escaped her and mixed with the lively sound of the music.

After only minutes, I was already getting that tingle all over my body. If I didn't control myself, I would lose it, and I didn't want this to end. I wanted it to last, so I slowed my pace, giving her those long dick strokes.

Pulling all the way out so that the head was at her opening, and then sinking into her.

I was fading into a haze, losing it again when her small hand slapped the counter and she yelled my name followed by a slew of elongated curse words and hisses.

"Aaron!"

She was close. Her body trembled against mine, fighting what was inevitable. When she started throwing her ass back against my dick, I knew she was on the brink of losing herself to the breathtaking rush of her orgasm.

It never failed, if she came, the tightening of her silky walls around my dick was guaranteed to drive me over the edge too. God, she was so fucking wet and tight. Her shit was always snug no matter how hard or how often I fucked her.

"Cum, Megan, please. I don't know how much longer I can take it. Your pussy... Fuck! It's so fucking good."

Then, like the good little vixen she was and without hearing me over the music, she came. She came hard, all over my dick. Her pussy massaged my dick into oblivion and drove me stark raving mad in the process.

The sensation bowed my back like I'd been struck by an unseen force of nature. Finally, I let go with a loud throat-scratching roar and fell against her back, still pumping into her.

***

After that better-than-drugs kind of sex, it was dinner and a movie. I was not much for watching anything but sports, but if Megan wanted to watch a movie, I sat and pretend to watch it along with her.

What I was doing was resting and storing up my energy for the next round. Like now, I'd seen enough of the beginning of the movie to remember who was starring in it, a little of the middle revealed who had gotten killed. Before the credits rolled, I'd watched the sappy ending.

Taking hold of one of Megan's feet, I began massaging it. "That was good," I stated, referring to the movie and not doing a good job of sounding convincing. She smiled at my unenthusiastic comment but didn't say anything.

Her mind had drifted, and her eyes told the story she hadn't yet revealed to me fully. There were times when her eyes would go empty like her body was present, but her mind had crept into the darkness and lingered there. I knew that darkness well enough to know that if you let it take you enough, there wouldn't be much of you left.

Megan had to be mentally drained after telling me the horror she lived through in her younger years, but there was still something missing. Of all the information I gathered from Megan's past when I was tracking her, after talking to the cigarette-smoking tit flasher, her friends from her old neighborhood that she believed I killed, and after Megan told me her story herself, I still sensed something was still off with her.

"I'm going to go take a shower," she announced before springing from the couch. It almost seemed like she sensed what I was thinking.

Thoughts running wild or not, they didn't stop me from admiring her ass while she walked away. This woman would be the death of me if I didn't watch myself.

Every time she uttered a word about leaving me, I made up any excuse to convince her to stay. *"One more day. Your mind needs to rest,"* I would plead, and she would give in. She was running from something, but what?

What could have possibly been worse than a serial-killing rapist foster father who not only raped her but forced her, an underage girl, to participate in his vicious slayings and somehow convinced her that it was her fault? I needed to find out what other secrets Megan was running from. If there was more to the story of what had happened to her in Texas, it couldn't have been good.

***

I floated someplace between this world and the next. I could hear myself moan, but my senses hadn't fully committed to being awake yet. My eyes snapped open, and the view of my bedroom ceiling filled my vision.

When I dropped my gaze lower, the view of Megan's hot wet mouth sliding over the swollen head of my dick made me shiver, and my breath got caught in my throat. Her full, supple lips spread to accommodate my dick and allowed it to slide deeper into her warm mouth. I stopped my hissing breaths so that I could allow the pleasure to sink into me uninterrupted.

What a fucking way to wake up. *This woman...* If angels or demons decided to come and drag my soul to hell right now, I would die a happy man.

"Fuck. That's it, baby," I encouraged. The job she was doing on my dick was so good I had to stop drool from drizzling out of my mouth. I chased every breath and feared I'd lost control of my left leg.

The leg dangled over the edge of the bed, and I was too overwhelmed to figure out if it had gone numb or if it was tingling under the influence of sex. It was a good sign that there was still movement in it. My damn toes were pointed to the ceiling, and if I didn't move them sometime soon, they'd probably end up stuck that way.

Megan fondled my balls and jiggled them, while simultaneously sending my dick sliding to the back of her throat and amplifying my high. I was losing my fucking mind. How she kept her mouth so wet with moisture, I had no idea. My eyes rolled to the top of my head, and like my stuck toes, I couldn't bring them down.

"Does that feel good?" Her warm breath vibrated over my dick. Her smooth voice was all that brought me out of my trance. She had no idea that her question had likely saved me from becoming cross-eyed and saved my damn toes from breaking off.

"Fuck, yes. It feels like fucking magic. Don't stop," I answered, my voice so heavy with lust, it didn't sound like my own.

Although my fingers sank into her curls, I didn't nudge her head down on my dick like I did with so many other women. She was doing such a good job on her own, she didn't need my assistance.

At times, it seemed Megan knew my body better than I did. The first two weeks she spent with me when she was working for my MC, she told me that she was studying me because she wanted to remember me. The lessons she'd given herself had paid off because she knew how to ease my damn mind clean out of my head.

My fingers tangled in her hair, giving me something to keep me tethered to this world. Megan had me. She had me so good, I didn't give one good goddamn how far removed she took me from the world as I knew it.

I couldn't talk. I couldn't breathe. I couldn't even fucking scream to save myself. When everything including my scalp and my toes began to tingle, and my damn soul acted like it wanted to uproot itself from my body, I couldn't do shit but moan and cry out.

It was this overpowering stimulant that kicked off my downward spiral straight into Megan's world. She'd taken me and locked me down and didn't even know it. I watched silently with a big-ass smile on my face as she threw away the fucking key so that I would never escape her.

Even if Megan didn't know it, I did. She was it for me. I was done. I was never going to fuck any other woman if it wasn't her. I wasn't going to want any other touching me. Hell, I didn't even want them looking at me.

When the smoke cleared, and I could wiggle my toes, open my eyes, and see straight again, it was her beautiful face smiling down at me.

Chapter Twenty-three

Megan

"Megan!" Aaron called me from his living room. He sounded impatient like he'd called for me several times before, but my mind had latched onto what I was doing.

"Yes? I'm coming," I called back to him as I reluctantly stepped away from his laptop that he rarely used. Since he snatched me from my condo without my laptop, I used his when my brain became oversaturated with random ideas that I needed to dispel through writing.

We were heading to the store to pick up a few supplies after I let Aaron talk me into staying with him throughout the weekend. I was lying to him. I didn't want to lie, but I told him that I would come back to him willingly if he let me go long enough to relocate and settle into my new place.

When he'd tracked me to my condo a few weeks ago, I was a few days away from moving. This move would be the most drastic I'd undertaken. I finally decided it was time I left the country altogether. Before Aaron came for me, I was in the process of finalizing my plans to move to the Dominican Republic since hopping my way across the United States didn't feel as safe as it once did.

If I left Aaron this time, I had to make sure he never found me again. I couldn't return to him no matter how badly every cell in my body ached for him. I couldn't let my past catch up with me and get Aaron caught in a fire-storm meant for me.

If I didn't leave Florida and soon, it would be too late to protect Aaron from shit that I had stirred. He lived a dangerous life, but I embraced danger too. Although I was only twenty-four, I had flirted with and lived with danger for a decade.

Aaron wasn't stupid. He knew that I hadn't told him everything, so he continued to subtly ask me questions, trying to figure out what else I was hiding from him.

"You're quieter than usual. You okay?" he asked. I sat slumped in the seat across from him with my head leaning against the headrest. The vibration of the speeding truck along the smooth path of the road relaxed me.

"I'm okay. Just thinking," I answered absently.

"What are you thinking about?" He asked. His tone was filled with patience and calm that didn't match his personality. The tolerance and care he was taking with me during and after my breakdown was a blessing I never ex-pected. He kept proving that he truly did care for me.

After all the shit I pulled, he'd managed to cast aside his anger, his ego, and irritation to take care of me. His actions made me love him even more.

I couldn't tell him I was sitting there thinking about leaving him and never returning. For a crazy-ass reason I had yet to figure out, I made the man happy. I failed to understand how two people who were outwardly polar op-posites, could be so compatible and likeminded. He understood me, and if I were willing to let him, I believed he would enter the gates of hell with me because hell was my final destination.

A storm was coming for me. I sensed it like old folks sensed rain, and I wanted to be as far away from Aaron as I could get when it hit. When I took too long to answer, he glanced in my direction.

"My MC wasn't the only group you've infiltrated, was it?"

I shook my head and swallowed hard, unwilling to go where his question might lead.

"How many others have there been? How many other groups have you manipulated?"

"Four." My hoarse tone barely carried over the hum of the truck. I was ashamed of myself for being this way, but I didn't know any other way.

"Fuck, Megan! Are you trying to get yourself killed? You have to stop this shit. It's only a matter of time before you get yourself into a situation you can't get out of."

I was already in a situation I couldn't get out of and I didn't want him to be dragged into it. He shook his head as his fists tightened around the steering wheel.

"Is this the reason you're anxious to move away from Florida? Because four dangerous groups of people may be after you at any given moment?"

"Well…I faked my death a couple of times, so only *two groups* of dangerous people may be after me."

My lack of emotion about what I'd done caused the crease between his eyes to deepen. He sighed and rubbed his forehead. He didn't know what to say to me after my comment.

Participating in violence with his MC and the notion that Aaron had a weakness for me were likely the only reasons I remained breathing. That being said, I couldn't let anything happen to Aaron because of me. I was finally accepting the cold, hard truth—I loved him.

***

It had taken about thirty minutes to shop for the groceries and personal items we needed. Aaron loaded the bags into the bed of his truck and shut the metal bed cover over the items. As soon as I climbed into his truck and shut the passenger's door, Aaron's frantic shout pierced my ears.

"Megan, get down!"

Aaron's booming voice scared the piss out of me. I craned my neck, jerking it from left to right, attempting to figure out what the hell was going on. My fingers dug into the headrest as I peeked around it, but nothing behind the truck that justified Aaron's shouts came into view.

All that followed was a quick angry burst of *Bam! Bam! Bam! Pop! Pop! Pop!*

The passenger's side mirror exploded into pieces, encouraging me to finally get my ass down like Aaron had ordered. My frantic wide eyes saw nothing but the ceiling and leather seat back of the truck's interior as I failed to catch the breaths that tore harshly from my overworked lungs.

My neck jerked in Aaron's direction when he snatched the driver's side door open and hopped inside.

He jammed the keys in the ignition and threw the truck into reverse after it roared to life.

I didn't know where he'd gotten a gun, but one sat wobbling across his lap as he slammed his foot down on the accelerator, sending the truck flying in reverse.

In my low crouch on the floor, I slammed into the glove box, but I was more concerned about what was happening outside than being tossed around inside the truck. Aaron half ducked while twisting his neck to glance back to see where he was directing the truck.

A loud *clap* rattled the back window, cracking it but not breaking it. Instinctively, I closed my eyes when pieces of glass rained down on me from someplace inside the truck. A powerful *whack* brought the truck to a sudden stop, sending me plowing into the seat bottom.

The engine released a loud scream as Aaron attempted to drive the accelerator through the floor to get us moving again. An elongated scratch of metal against metal filled my ears followed by a loud knocking sound that made the truck rear up. We ran over something I believed was meant to keep us immobile. We may have even hit a person.

Just as fast as Aaron had put the truck in reverse, he threw it into drive and stomped on the accelerator again. All while, what I assumed were bullets, pelted the outside of the truck's body.

I cringed and drew into a tighter ball with each thump, my desperate eyes remained wide as my brain conjured up answers.

I believe my past had finally caught up with me, and Aaron was likely going to pay the price for being with me.

His body twisted all over the place. With roving eyes and erratic neck movements, he checked the rearview and driver's side mirrors before turning and angling his body so he could glance back through the cracked back window.

We were moving at a rate well past the speed limit, and the swish of vehicles sounded as we zoomed past them. I rocked back and forth and side to side with every sharp twist Aaron made on the steering wheel.

The engine roared like a lion in full stride. We moved at a break-neck pace, and I didn't know if whoever was shooting at us was still chasing us or if Aaron had lost them.

"Megan, reach in the glove box and get me another gun and extra clips," he instructed as his eyes continued to scan the view in front, behind, and on the sides of us.

I started to rise from my spot on the floor so I could open the glove box, but Aaron's firm hand landed on my shoulder and stopped me.

"Stay down. These motherfuckers are right on our ass." His harsh breathing competed with the engine's growl as he worked to keep us safe and out of danger.

I leaned back against the seat to get the glove box open. A Beretta, a Glock-17, and from my dimmed view, what I believed was a HK45 rested inside the glove box. Counting the .45 Aaron had sitting on his lap, there were four guns in the cab of this truck.

After handing Aaron the extra .45 and four loaded clips of extra ammunition, I took the Beretta for myself before I shut the glove box.

Seeing all those guns reminded me that Aaron lived a life as dangerous as mine, and in the short time I'd gotten to know him, I knew that guns were a part of his norm.

Just when I allowed myself to think that things were calming, I went lurching into the edge of the seat before I went sliding sideways in the opposite direction toward Aaron's feet. Someone had slammed into the back of us.

Chapter Twenty-four

Megan

The squeal and stutter of the tires reached me as I gripped the seat cushion to stay upright. My fingers clawed into the upholstery like a frantic cat being lowered into a pool of water.

Aaron had turned onto what I assumed was a dirt road. It wasn't as rutty or bumpy as the road to his house, but we'd left the smooth surface of asphalt.

An unfamiliar sound made my ears perk up. A crunching noise registered, but it wasn't rocks that the wheels crushed as we bounced about.

"If they come into these woods, they better know them better than me," Aaron muttered, glancing back.

His statement let me know that we'd entered the woods and it was twigs snapping under the tires as we drove. Although the windows were rolled most of the way up, I could still make out the low whine of insects and the sweet melody of birds' songs welcoming us. The earthy scent that crept into the truck's interior was another clue that we were under the cover of leaves and branches.

Aaron was betting on knowing these woods well enough to beat whoever the hell was chasing us. He was leading those who hunted us *out back*. If there was one thing Copper County had a lot of, it was *out back*.

After minutes of bouncing over the rugged terrain of the wooded path we'd taken, the view that swallowed us was of trees whose willowy limbs, heavy trunks, and fat shimmering leaves allowed only flickers of light to peek through. Leaves and pebbles rained down on the truck as we rolled toward our destination.

The sun was already making its descent since it was late evening, and its orange glow made it look like we were on the reverse side of a nature painting. The deeper we went, the darker my wooded view grew.

The thickening of the trees dimmed the light and allowed darkness to take over. Another sharp turn sent me careening again before the squeak of the brakes brought the truck to a sudden stop.

"Come on, Megan, follow me," Aaron called back after he slung his squeaking door open.

The first thing I did was grab the gun I took from the glove compartment before I climbed into the seat, hopped over the center console, and followed Aaron out of his door.

He shoved one of his guns down the back of his jeans and kept the other aimed and ready to shoot.

"I saw you take a gun. You still have it?" he asked without glancing down at me.

"Yes," I answered, my breaths rushing too fast out of my mouth as my feet raked over the grass and twig-lined surface below.

"Good girl," he called back to me as he took off toward the back of his truck.

He opened the bed cover of his truck, reached in blindly and dragged out a large duffle bag. He slung the bag over his shoulder and left the hatch of his truck open. He walked back to me, adjusting an object in his hand. When he shut the driver's side truck door behind me, the interior light went off, leaving us in darkness.

"Let's go. Stay close," he directed. "If you see anyone that's not me, shoot the motherfucker."

"Okay," I said without protest. However, I did consider how the hell I was supposed to shoot at anything in the dark? The night hadn't fully possessed the day, but the trees were thick enough to cast our surroundings in enough shadow that it may as well have been night.

Aaron navigated the dark, uneven terrain smoothly. Insects continued to call even as my trampling steps disturbed their homes. Although Aaron wore heavy boots, his footsteps were as light as a sneaky cat's.

We hiked about two hundred paces away from the truck before Aaron directed me into a dugout or ditch. How he saw anything was beyond me because I could hardly see my shadowy hands in front of my face.

"Here, Megan, lay here flat on your stomach. I'll help you put these on."

I climbed into the hole, which wasn't as deep as the dark view had led me to believe it was. About two or two and a half feet deep, the hole was wide and long enough for me to fit and lay comfortably inside.

The soft roar of engines and the crunch of twigs and leaves snapping under tires alerted us that multiple vehicles were approaching. I couldn't tell if there were two vehicles or five, but I was certain there was more than one.

They must have cut their headlights off because the engine noises indicated they were close, but I didn't see any visible light.

When Aaron slipped something plastic and metal over my head and dropped it over my eyes, I didn't move. I didn't even breathe because I had no idea what was happening until he flipped a switch. A low wheezing sounded before my dark view turned into a green one.

Night vision goggles? What the…?

This was how Aaron could see. What was he doing with this type of equipment?

Careful twig-breaking footsteps and the unmistakable *clicks* of weapons being charged was what funneled into my ears. Sounds were different here in the woods—more sharp, crisp, and distinct.

Aaron placed my hand on what I discerned was a metal knob.

"Adjust the sight using this knob. Stay low and if it doesn't look like me, aim for the head in case they're wearing armor, and don't hesitate. *Shoot*," he instructed in a low tone.

Before I could get a word out, he was climbing out of the hole. The night goggles gave me the ability to see him running back toward his truck or toward what could well have been an army of men.

The view through the goggles was green, glowing, and unsteady, and I didn't know enough about them to know if this view was normal or if it needed further adjusting. Nothing had distinct or crisp shapes or colors. Everything was glow-light green and floated across my vision.

"Fuck," I murmured when something slithered across the backside of one of my legs. My teeth sank deep into my bottom lip before I went stock still. Thank God, I'd changed into jeans. Wasn't that the rambling sounds of a fight in the background? However, I was distracted by the creature on my leg.

I didn't know if what had crawled onto me was a snake, a rat, or some other woodland creature that ate human flesh. A stabbing chill ran up my spine, and I fought a shiver as the thing lingered at the back of my left thigh. Was it burrowing itself into my leg? I exploded with panic, wanting to jump up and scream, but forcing myself to remain in place.

Fuck! Fuck! Fuck! What is it?

Adrenaline pumped through me so thickly, I became one massive heartbeat. I couldn't help my reaction. I couldn't lie there and give the thing time to decide what part of my leg it wanted to take a chunk out of.

I heaved my body sideways, gritting my teeth with the force and effort I put into the turn. My movement sent whatever the hell it was on my leg someplace else. My ears perked at the sound of it scurrying away, its claws scratching the ground as it ran into the darkness.

As soon as I was rid of my attacker, a loud series of body damaging cracks sounded in the distance. I nearly twisted my neck off my shoulders, from snapping around to scan for the location of the sound. I prayed it wasn't Aaron who was on the wrong side of those bone-breaking strikes.

Loud angry grunts sent my head to the back of Aaron's truck. Two green figures were back there, fighting.

Their loud heaves and grunts echoed through the dark. Their pounding fists connected with flesh and registered even louder as the two glowing green masses continued to scuffle.

I didn't know if it was instinct or blind luck, but when the hairs on the back of my neck stood like a ghostly hand had passed across them, I turned and found a green form creeping its way in my direction with his weapon aimed and at the ready. Aaron's sharp words replayed in my brain, *"If you see anyone that's not me, shoot."*

So, I aimed. And I shot. The person went still before they dropped to their knees. They gripped their neck. A gurgling sound followed, confirming that I shot them in a place that affected their breathing. I lifted the gun to shoot again, but the body tumbled forward and remained still. To make sure he stayed down, I shot again at the unmoving mass on the ground.

I turned back to the fight still in progress behind the truck. Since it was difficult to tell one person from the next, I was clueless as to who was winning the fight, Aaron or the bad guy.

An unworldly squeal sounded and brought my stabbing chill right back. One of the green figures repeatedly jammed a sharp instrument that must have been a knife, into the head and neck region of the other man.

A loud throat rattling *humph* followed each stab. The stabber kept stabbing until his adversary stopped making sounds and then hunched low next to the victim. The only logical explanation was that it was Aaron waiting for the rest of them.

My nerves were wound so tightly, I didn't bother to slap away a buzzing insect as it fussed near my ear. My roving eyes remained on who I convinced myself was Aaron until he eased up and ran deeper into the woods. His silent stride didn't match the energetic movement of his body. The large dark body of the truck obstructed him the further away he went, causing him to disappear from my view.

A quiet moment that lasted a lifetime passed before an eerie series of moans floated through the darkness, but there were no green figures in sight for me to match with the sound. The sound grew more intense and heart wrenching. The haunting cries filled the air with a creepy stillness that had goose bumps running up my arms. I knew that sound. I'd heard it before. *A death moan*. Someone was dying, and I prayed it wasn't Aaron.

On the verge of calling out to him, I pinched my lips shut. My eagerness to go searching for him intensified, but I fought it and inched lower behind the packed dirt of my hiding place. I burned with the need to see if Aaron was okay, but I had to believe that he was alive.

Another moment of chilling silence enveloped the woods. The insects stopped singing, the animals stopped calling, and even the leaves had stopped their low chorus of swaying melodies. I held my breath for what had to be a lifetime as only the sound of my fluttering heart registered.

Chapter Twenty-five

Aaron

Leaving Megan in that dugout wasn't easy but necessary. Also, I knew that she wouldn't hesitate to put a bullet in a motherfucker if she needed to. The wailing cackle of a noisy bird helped conceal my cover as I crept back toward my truck. Once I reached the back, I dropped into a prone position and crawled under the ass end of the bed. It was too bad I hadn't had time to put my sniper rifle together.

Two SUV's had come to a stop about fifty paces away from my truck. So far, I counted five, positioning themselves in various areas around my vehicle and theirs. Their tactical movements and the silencers on their weapons drew my focus. They were either trained by a secret militia or were prior military or law enforcement.

They fanned out, hoping to surround me and Megan, but all they were doing was making my job easier.

I could clearly see two, sweeping the area, their guns aimed and ready to blow a hole in me. They wore night gear which meant they were likely hired guns with access to gear and equipment that was not easily accessible to the general public.

I inched my head back under the tail end of my truck when one crept in my direction. He was clueless as to where I was and made no attempt to quiet his steps as he hiked closer to me, looking in every direction. When he went up on his toes, I knew he was glancing over and into the raised bed of my truck.

He hadn't looked down, which was good news for me. I was about to expose myself for an ambush, but keeping them away from Megan was my main goal.

My arm snaked out from the darkness of my hiding place, and I gripped the man's ankle when his leg passed within my reach. Down he went with a loud *humph*. Within seconds, I was on him, attacking with punches and beating him about the head with the butt of my weapon. I was reluctant to fire my weapon since it wasn't silenced, but the man was a fighter.

He stopped my attempts to disarm him of his gun and blocked the blow I sent at his jaw. I swiveled nearly in a circle around him while staying clear of the barrel of his weapon that had let off two silenced rounds that sped past my head and went into the air. The hot lead of one of the bullets had passed so close to my head, I swear I saw the trail of fire chasing the projectile into the darkness.

Just as the man attempted to inch his finger down on the trigger again, I trapped his arm with mine and hammered the gun from his tight grip. He sent an uppercut to my nose, sending my head back with a hard jerk that nearly snapped my neck. Blood dripped from my nose as the blow blurred my vision for a second.

My elbow went flying into the man's jaw. We tousled, dueling like warriors for the upper hand. We remained tangled up like two riled up snakes rolling around on the ground.

The man's hand-to-hand combat skills were just as good as mine, but I didn't have time to trade rounds with him. I allowed him a few free blows to my face while I retrieved my hunting knife from my waistband. The bastard blocked my first attempt at sending the knife into his face, but my second attempt sliced across his shoulder inflicting minimal damage because of the thick armored vest he wore.

The sound of a gunshot from my rear caught my attention. It could only have been Megan shooting since this crew had silencers attached to their weapons. My intent was to run toward her, but I spotted two more heading in her direction if I didn't keep them distracted.

Out of the corner of my eye, I saw one of the two I'd spotted turn in my direction, taking careful steps so as not to call our attention as I battled with his buddy for supremacy. The knowledge that I was about to be double teamed shot an extra spark of strength into me.

I jammed my free hand under the man's shoulder and twisted hard to turn him. Once I had his swarming body turned just right, I placed my knee to his back, and I forced his face into the ground. With one hand available, I gave my knife a little toss to reposition it before jamming it into the man's neck. Body shots weren't going to penetrate the vest, so head and neck shots were my only options.

The stab shocked the man, but he was a tough bastard who wasn't going down easily. His friend continued to creep in our direction as we tussled, no doubt assuming I hadn't noticed him attempting to use the tree trunks as cover.

I rolled away from the one who gave my knife a resting place in his neck and gripped the gun that I had hammered out of his tight grip. With a steady aim, I remained low to the ground. I pointed the silenced weapon at the approaching man and didn't hesitate to fire since he was aiming and ready to fire on me.

The first two slugs sent him stumbling back on unsteady legs, but he didn't fall. The third shot froze him in place for a few seconds before his body teetered forward and fell stiffly to the ground.

My small victory wasn't going to be celebrated because the tough bastard I stabbed had jerked my knife from his neck and was climbing over my prone body. He rained down punches to the side of my head and back of my neck. I bucked like a wild boar attempting to get him off me.

My concentration was poured into getting my hand on the wound I inflicted to his neck.

Once I managed to flip onto my side and forced my hand through the barrage of punches he was landing, my fingers slipped and slid over his bloody neck until my thumb slipped into the knife wound.

The man released a loud squeal, and I took advantage of his weak state by using his head for a punching bag. I increased the pressure of my thumb pressing into his knife wound. My thumb was shoved into his neck down to the knuckle as I tried to rip his flesh apart.

I lost the silenced pistol I used to take out his friend and had no idea where my own gun had ended up. My lips twitched into a smile when my sweeping knee rubbed across a hard metal object.

My knife.

My eager hand gripped my knife as I swiveled my hips and overpowered the man enough to straddle him. Aiming for his throat, I repeatedly stabbed him delivering each blow with maximum force. Each stab I delivered was followed up by a loud gurgling grunt from the man's damaged throat.

"Die already, motherfucker," I hissed between clenched teeth while continuing to plunge the knife into his neck. The sinewy texture of his flesh and tendons as the blade ripped and tore through them felt familiar. The tip of the knife vibrated against bone chipping off fragments as I continued to plunge the knife into his neck and face, unable to but wanting to see the true level of damage I was doing to this asshole. Finally, after the eleventh stab, the tension in his body released and his arms fell limp to the ground.

With Megan on my mind, I ran out into the opening between the first SUV and my truck and immediately started taking on gunfire. The darkness and me wearing night goggles were the only reasons I was able to contend with this group.

I dived behind a tree in the nick of time as more bullets striking at the opposite side hit with deadly impact. My back kissed its scaly body as I inched up the thick bark of the tree.

After shoving the gun into the back of my pants, I fell forward, catching myself when the palms of my hands broke the fall. Aligning my movement with the thick bark of the tree, I crawled away on my belly hoping the men hadn't spotted me approaching the next set of thick trees that lined the woods like a burly squad of dark soldiers. With multiple branches to keep me hidden, my intention was to make the task of them finding me more difficult.

No sooner than I thought it, snapping twigs alerted me to someone's approach. One was at the tree I'd just left. Crouched low to the ground, I chanced a quick peek and noticed the figure was peeking around the tree, searching for me.

I side eyed the other as he attempted to creep up behind me. They were laying a trap. A sinister smile crept across my lips at knowing their tactics.

Certain that he hadn't spotted me yet, I placed my back to the one in front of me, the tree keeping me concealed, as I aimed at the one who believed he was about to sneak up on me. They apparently didn't know I was wearing night goggles.

With the silenced pistol from the one I stabbed, I fired three consecutive shots in the direction of the one approaching me from the rear. One of the bullets landed in a vital area that caused him to stumble and halt his approach.

The loud and forceful snaps and thump of bullets hitting the tree revealed that the other man was barreling toward me. The thick bark of the tree kept me safe from the stream of rounds being released as the man's angry roar echoed throughout the woods.

As soon as he paused, I reached around the fat trunk of the tree and fired. One, two, three shots didn't take him down. I was unable to get off a good enough shot to hit him where it would hurt.

He roared toward me, ducking and zigzagging as the pistol in my hand made a snapping noise. He continued to let his finger snag at the trigger on reflex. We were both out of ammunition.

I dropped the useless gun and flung my blade with as much force as I could muster, catching him in the face or neck. The man's squeal livened up the woods, quieting the animals and insects. He was close enough that his wild howl escaped through an opening other than his mouth.

The horror riding his voice was laced with a hair-raising shriek that only came from the dying. I remained behind the cover of the tree in case his last thoughts were to take me to hell with him.

His cries finally turned into a moan that crept through the darkness and made you pause to listen. I recalled hearing that type of distressed moan many times before. It meant that death was standing at the man's shoulders and so was I a few seconds later.

After relieving him of his gun that he'd let slip from his trembling hand, I kneeled over him, bearing witness to death dragging that bastard's soul straight to hell.

He made the fatal mistake of following me into these woods to take Megan's life and mine. Therefore, I didn't have an ounce of remorse for his suffering. I yanked my knife from his twitching neck and the drip drops of blood hitting the ground registered before the rusted scent snuck up my nostrils.

I focused on the part of his face I could see in the darkness before I placed my hand over his mouth and nose. The air I blocked from passing through his nose and quivering lips hissed out of the hole my knife had left in his neck.

With the strength he had left, he clawed at my hand and scratched at my arm, but he was too weak to do anything but lie there and allow me to assist death in getting him to hell faster.

Megan and I were the hunted now. Other than the one I was confident she had killed, there were at least two more of these assholes out here. The eerie silence let me know that they were hiding, biding their time until Megan and I revealed ourselves. But there was one thing they hadn't counted on or simply didn't know. I knew these woods. I hunted in these woods. I buried bodies in these woods. The hole I hid Megan in was supposed to be a grave for a man I decided to let live because he would suffer more alive.

It took precious time, but patience landed me on the trail of one. Although I possessed a certain level of confidence that she could take care of herself, I also felt guilty about dragging her into this by not letting her leave the many times she'd asked.

This was the second time the dangerous life I led had put her life in serious jeopardy. No wonder the woman wanted to move away from Florida so badly. Maybe I was reading too much into her actions by thinking she was running from something. Maybe I just needed an excuse to keep her instead of letting her go. Maybe she was just a woman haunted by her past, who, by unconventional means, had tried to fix herself.

A sliver of movement caught my eye. Death was in my corner this night with a spit bucket and a towel as he cheered me on. Another enemy had revealed his position. A smile glided across my lips and vanished when another gun blast sounded. It could have only been Megan firing off another shot.

My anxiety shot through the roof. I couldn't just get up and run toward her because of the asshole limping into my direction with his weapon raised. With most of his friend's dead, he was liable to fire at anything that moved.

With my weapon drawn up to my chest, I prepared to step out and shoot. The element of surprise should give me at least a second or two of reaction time.

"Fuck," I mouthed silently as the light steps the man attempted to take stopped. My eyes widened behind the lens of the goggles as I peeked over my shoulder, around the tree and drew my head back as quickly when hot lead flew in my direction.

The tough bark of the tree dug into my back, protecting me from the onslaught of oncoming gunfire. This asshole was determined to kill me, but his ammunition was not going to last forever.

A three second pause was long enough for me to believe that the shooter was dropping and reloading a magazine. I spun away from my cover, blasting his ass. Bullet after bullet struck him, sending his body back violently.

One of the bullets made such a hard impact, his pistol went flying south, clanking to the ground. Since his body armor had stopped my bullets from damaging his body, I stabbed him with my knife, sending it plunging into the side of his face when he turned at the last minute. The blade collided with his teeth, causing the man to release an ear-splitting howl of pain, but also stopping the level of damage I intended to inflict.

Retracting my blade quickly, blood gushed from his jaw. Despite his injury, he still attempted to slap a new magazine into his weapon, but his attempt was useless as I spun, giving the knife maximum force as it plunged into his neck to the hilt. His legs gave and his body jerked and convulsed, struggling to fight off his impending death.

His mouth remained open as desperate gasps escaped his throat. After retracting it, I jammed the blade in once more, twisting and forcing it upward as the wet sound of ripping flesh floated through the air.

I left the man twitching on the ground and ran toward Megan, praying and hoping she'd defended herself like I know she could.

Chapter Twenty-six

Megan

A series of gunshots sounded, and all I could make out were flashes on the far side of Aaron's truck. A hair-raising roar sounded that made my lips twitch with a smile.

I would recognize Aaron's roar anywhere. The scuffing and body-shaking strikes indicated another fight.

How many guys were out there? From my location, it was hard to tell how many vehicles had driven up.

Heavy steps beat rapidly against the uneven, leaf and twig-littered ground. Someone was running, and the sound was growing close enough for me to make out the rasp of their winded breathing.

They were at my back, so I flipped my weapon and aimed toward the approaching noise. When the green form came into view, I was hesitant to shoot because I didn't know if it was Aaron or one of the bad guys.

There was no way this guy was six-feet-two, but he was close enough to discover my hiding spot. My grip tightened around the stiff metal in my hand before my finger flexed against the trigger.

Bam!

The shot rang out loud and long and hovered in the air above me. The bullet struck the man someplace in the upper torso where the impact snatched him back.

A series of guttural grunts sounded before the second bullet struck him in the head, from me squeezing the trigger instinctively when he didn't go down fast enough.

Green sparks of what must have been blood flew into the air, and his body followed as it fell back and hit the ground with a final *thump*.

Heavy steps beat angrily at the ground behind me and sent me back onto my stomach as my head darted toward Aaron's truck. Another green form was heading my way at an alarming pace. I raised my gun, prepared to shoot, but resisted the urge to pull the trigger. This guy was damn sure over six feet, but was it Aaron?

"Megan. Are you okay?"

Sweet relief swept through me at the sound of Aaron's voice. He was alive, and thankfully, I hadn't mistakenly shot him.

"I'm okay," I called back to him, unsure if we were alone or still under attack.

I jumped when Aaron's firm grip reached through the darkness and wrapped around my forearm. He lifted me out of that ditch like my five-foot-five, one-hundred and thirty-pound body was nothing more than a small sack of potatoes.

No sooner had he released me, and my feet were planted on the ground did I hear the familiar sound of him slapping another clip into one of the guns he carried.

"Let's go. I think they're all dead."

Think?

The night goggles had slipped from my eyes when Aaron yanked me up. I held the gear to my face with one hand, and the warm gun swung in my other as I jogged to keep up with Aaron's quick steps.

He yanked his driver's side door open, and I blindly stepped onto the running board before swinging my gun hand into the seat, unwilling to let go of the gun. I climbed over the center console and shoved the night goggles off my head since they were lopsided on my face.

The flash of headlights and the roar of a vehicle's engine breathed new life into the dark, leafy woods and sent both my and Aaron's wide gazes in the direction of the light.

I lowered in the seat, but my eyes remained peeled. What was that vehicle going to do?

Instead of remaining inside the truck with me, Aaron hopped out and took quick steps to the back of his truck. The headlights allowed me to peek and see the top of Aaron's head at the back of his truck. He was back there, fixing or maneuvering a large object. I could hear the unmistakable clink of metal.

My brain froze when he left the cover of the back of his truck and took off running toward the headlights whose brightness made him a clear target. Aaron believed they were all dead. Was the driver unarmed? Injured? Was that the reason he wasn't shooting at Aaron or attempting to run him down with the vehicle?

The bright light was directly in front of him now. Aaron's shadow danced behind his urgent movements as he inched closer to the dark colored SUV.

The driver revved the engine, but Aaron didn't move. He stood there prepared to go head-to-head with two or more tons of revved up metal.

My mouth dropped wide open and utter disbelief hit my system when my eyes latched onto the object Aaron had pointed at the vehicle. He was out there with a fucking grenade launcher. At least it was what I believed it was called. I could plainly see him shift and adjust something on the large weapon. It was as thick as his muscular arm but longer.

He lifted the thing over his shoulder and fired it as the vehicle's tires scratched into the dirt in an attempt to move away from Aaron at a fast rate of speed in reverse.

A loud swishing noise came from the weapon, followed by a whistling sound that floated through the sky, chasing down the vehicle.

Aaron immediately dropped to the ground, respecting what came out of that weapon more than the vehicle that could have run him over. The SUV had taken off, rolling in reverse to get away from what could only be described as flying death, but it was too late.

Although I couldn't see it traveling through the sky, the grenade made a direct impact with the vehicle because the *boom* shook Aaron's truck and vibrated the glass so hard, I ducked, thinking the blast would bust out the windows.

The vehicle exploded into a mass of burning flames that lit up the woods and spewed thick, black, billowing smoke. I rose in time to see Aaron running back my way. Aware that we needed to get away, I climbed over the console, stomped on the brake and attempted to start the truck. Its engine stuttered for a few scary seconds but roared to life.

Once Aaron reached the back of his truck, the loud *clink* of the weapon hitting the metal bed of the truck sounded before he slammed the cover shut. As soon as he climbed into the cab with me, Aaron shifted the truck into drive and sped off.

My neck twisted to keep the spectacle in my view when we passed the burning SUV. We sped over the untamed ground faster than we should have but with justifiable reasoning.

"That vehicle is going to attract a lot of attention. We need to get as far away from this shit as possible. The seven bodies we dropped are going to bring the feds and every other high-level law agency that believe they have jurisdiction," Aaron informed me while directing the truck and glancing back at the scene.

"Are you hurt?" he asked me, continuing to wheel the bouncing truck wildly.

"No," I answered. "Are you?"

"A few scratches, bumps, and bruises. Nothing life-threatening, though," he replied.

A long pause followed before I climbed atop the seat to be closer to him. I rested my head against Aaron's strong shoulder. My hand rested on his chest as my ass hung off the center console.

Our heart rates pumped as fast as the pistons under Aaron's hood, still amped up from our *out back* experience.

After our breathing finally calmed to steady breaths, the words, "I'm sorry, Aaron," fell out of my mouth.

While steering the truck through the last of the wooded terrain, he caressed my wrist before pulling my hand to his lips to place a quick kiss to the back of it.

"What are you sorry for?" he asked, glancing back once more through his cracked back window.

"Unless you know who those guys were, it's my fault that you had to kill them. They were probably after me, and now your life's in jeopardy. I can't let anything happen to you because of me."

"This is not your fault," he said with stern certainty in his tone. "Those guys could have been after me as much as they could have been after you. You remember what happened at my house a few days before you left. Chuck, Clint, and Dutch weren't there to hold hands and be friendly. My life teeters on the edge of death every day. I've been hanging on to death's fucking coattails since the day I was born."

He made a good point, but every instinct within me said those guys had caught up to me because I stayed in Florida too long. Aaron's voice drew my attention.

"When I do find out who the fuck it was, you'd better believe they are going to figure out that I'm not some backwoods redneck they can run all over."

I believed him. Anyone who carried around a fucking grenade launcher had undoubtedly seen more action, death, and destruction than I could have imagined.

Chapter Twenty-seven

Megan

The motel we checked into made the Bates Motel look like a five-star resort. We had driven over seventy miles away from the woods where Aaron and I had left seven dead bodies and a blown-up vehicle.

His shirt was soaked through with blood, enough that I had to cut him out of it. It wasn't until I began cutting his shirt away that the rusted scent of blood made its way up my nose and rested at the back of my throat.

During the seventy-mile drive, he'd not once complained about bleeding or pain and was more concerned about how I was doing than about his own health. The cheap motel contained rooms that faced woodland. This allowed us to park around the back of the building to hide Aaron's damaged and now suspect vehicle.

He'd been stabbed in his left side during one of his scuffles with the bad guys. The wound was deep enough that I suggested he go to the hospital, but Aaron wouldn't hear of it. Like the act was something simple, he insisted on coaching me on how to clean and sew him up.

There was no use in me arguing with him about it. Aaron would do whatever Aaron wanted to do. It hadn't taken me but a few quick interactions to know that he was an alpha male who wasn't going to bend to the whims and demands of the rest of the world.

However, there were moments when he dropped the armor and allowed me small peeks at the parts of him that I was certain no one else had ever seen.

Now, he was talking to his father on speakerphone while I tended to his wound.

"No, it was not the law," Aaron urged. He talked while his phone sat on the table next to us, but his encouraging eyes remained on my tense face while I played nurse.

"Are you sure it wasn't the Slimy Bastards? They've had a hard on for us for a while now."

Aaron shook his head.

"This was not another MC. Those motherfuckers had military-grade weapons. They were aiming to kill, and they didn't give a flying fuck about collateral damage. They opened fire in a grocery store parking lot. I had to lead them away from town. They didn't count on me having the kind of weaponry that could contend with theirs."

The sound of a weapon being charged on his father's end of the call hinted that Shark heeded Aaron's warning and was preparing for battle.

"So, what were they? Black, White, Mexican? Who the fuck are we dealing with? Can't be the Russians. We didn't leave a trail for them to connect the dots to us, right?"

Aaron glanced down at my work before he answered his father's question. "Spanish was being spoken and not the usual Spanglish mix they speak here in Florida. This group was Mexican and not Tex-Mex either. And fuck you. You know fucking well I took care of the Russians. They don't call me Grave Digger for nothing."

Grave Digger? I'm sleeping with someone known as Grave Digger?

My mind reeled at the conversation I was hearing between Aaron and his father. What the hell had I gotten myself into? I had seriously underestimated Aaron and his MC.

I knew the August Knights had a reputation. I knew Aaron was dangerous based on what had gone down at his house the first time I stayed with him. But, the things they were revealing now had elevated their danger status. Like getting away with killing Russians and a number of other groups based on their conversation. It left me thinking back to all those times Shark and Aaron kept warning me that they were dangerous people.

I used the old rusted hot plate and a small metal pot to boil water. The bubbling liquid from the steaming pot competed with the sound of the clunking air-conditioning unit, filling the stale air of the motel with its own harmony.

When a knock sounded at the door, Aaron had a weapon in his hand within seconds. His finger didn't ease away from the trigger until the person announced, "Front desk."

I had called down to the front desk and listened to the attendant grumble about having to bring us extra towels. Aaron pointed me to a hiding spot behind the bed before he shoved the pistol down the back of his pants. I remained hidden but couldn't help peeking above the lumpy mattress to see if it truly was the front desk.

When Aaron answered the door shirtless, the man's face went from sour to sunshine and sprinkles in seconds. His eyes lustfully traveled the expanse of Aaron's tempting body.

My first smile came at the sight of Aaron jerking the towels from the man's grasp and slamming the door in his smiling face.

Aaron didn't get the full gist of how much attention he could pull. When we were at any public place, smiles came easy, chests poked out further, and he was offered help when he didn't even need it. My smile deepened, now that I saw that not even men were immune to him.

The tattoos, the hair, his strong fit body, and those piercing, blue eyes could probably get him just about anything he wanted. Aaron had everything he needed to turn the most disciplined head, and I wasn't sure he realized it.

The motel's half-empty first aid kit contained items that appeared older than Aaron's twenty-seven and my twenty-four years combined. I poured the boiling water over the needle to sterilize it and wasn't entirely sure the old thread would knit Aaron's skin back together.

God, this man could take a lot of pain. He continued to make warning calls to his MC members as he directed me on how to clean and sew up his wound. Repeatedly shoving a tiny sliver of metal through human skin was more difficult than doctors made it look.

My hand shook less with each passage of the needle through Aaron's skin, but my thumb had gone numb from how hard I needed to push to break through his flesh. Aaron was calm enough for the both of us because I didn't relax until the last stitch.

"Done," I called, relieved that it was over.

When I turned to walk away to discard the trash and put up the supplies, Aaron gripped my wrist. He didn't have to utter a word to me. The firm grip of his fingers around my wrist and the glint of lust in his eyes expressed words he didn't have to speak. He swiped his phone off in the middle of someone talking.

My smile beamed down on him as I dropped the supplies on the rickety table next to us. I stepped between his splayed legs before I leaned down and placed a tender kiss on his lips. His hands raced up either side of me before my lips skimmed over his prickly jaw and sat on top of his ear.

"Let's shower first," I suggested, knowing damn well what showering with him would do. I glanced casually back at him as I headed toward the bathroom, putting a little extra sway in my hips.

Chapter Twenty-eight

Megan

Once in the bathroom, I drew back the shower curtain and paused when Aaron entered the bathroom after me. I waited until he was close enough for his warm breath to sweep across my face.

"You know, Aaron, thinking about you firing that grenade launcher has my pussy getting wetter by the second."

My comment made his smile spread. What the hell was wrong with me? My libido was out of control. I had no off switch when it came to Aaron. Him having a body that called to my every desire and a dick that could fill many women's fantasies added fuel to my amped-up desires.

Aaron didn't comment. He stepped into my personal space and bent slightly, lifting me. Automatically, my legs wrapped around his waist. The stitches I'd haphazardly sewn into his side came to mind, but Aaron didn't give a damn about those stitches.

He reached down and filled both his hands with my ass. My legs drew tighter around his waist until I was able to cross them at his lower back.

"You're going to bust your low budget stitches," I warned before smiling playfully at him.

He took my bottom lip first, sucking on it. A greedy kiss followed as he walked us closer to the shower. He reached in and twisted the shower knob without pulling his lips away from mine.

He waited until the water warmed, with me wrapped around him. His hands never stopped roaming my body, and in response, my hands roved freely over his strong chiseled chest and back.

I had taken inventory of his body and spotted multi-colored bruises on his arms, chest, and back, but like that stab wound, he didn't care. By the time steam misted from the shower, Aaron had steam rolling off me.

We hurriedly tore off the rest of our clothes and allowed the warm water to wash our sins down the drain. I took my time scrubbing him clean, and he had no problem allowing me to linger in the places I believed were the dirtiest. By the time I finished my cleaning, his dick was as stiff as the pipes spilling water on us.

Aaron ignored his obvious need and returned the favor. Strong hands washed me with slow soapy strokes that cleaned and massaged me at the same time. Our need grew more intense with each swipe of his hand over my body. When his finger brushed my warm, gushy center and slid inside me, my lips fell apart but my moan remained caught in my throat.

My eyes lingered on his straight white teeth as they sank into his tempting pink lips. The haze of his desire darkened, and his gaze loitered on mine while his fingers worked me into a frenzy. Next thing I knew, he lifted my semi-soapy body before backing me under the water to rinse me off.

Warm water beat against my skin, but it was nothing compared to the man standing between my legs. I gripped the back of his neck and one of his bulging biceps. My eyes didn't dare drop away from his until he filled me to the hilt, and I was forced to close them.

"Oh God. Aaron," I hissed out as my wet body shivered with pleasure.

It hadn't been a full day since we'd been together, but it seemed like weeks had passed. After the first thrust, he paused, savoring the delectable excitement that took our breaths and united us in a way that no one else would understand.

He backed out and heaved his dick back inside my pussy, repeating the action until I forgot about the shootout in the woods, the blown-up vehicle, or that anyone had even been aiming to kill us.

God. This man had complete possession of my mind and body. He took me to places I had never been, made me come alive with sensations I never knew existed, and could make me forget about the world outside and concentrate only on us.

After we managed to dry off our shaky post-orgasmic bodies, we stumbled to the lumpy bed and fell in, giggling about our inability to get enough of each other once we got started. It didn't take long for one of Aaron's strong hands to wrap around my ankle and for me to be dragged into position.

Neither of us cared what position we ended up in, as long as we were fucking the hell out of each other. I straddled his lap, my pussy dripping wet even after the wet episode in the shower. His hard dick dug into my stomach, its warm, velvety texture against my skin made its presence known.

I sprinkled kisses all over his face before I covered his lips with mine and searched for his tongue. Our tongues mated, sliding up and down and over and under as we feasted on each other.

The bags of food he'd taken out of the back of his truck bed were forgotten along with the duffle he dragged out of his truck. He said the duffle contained a fresh change of clothes.

He didn't need to tell it for me to know the duffle also contained more guns. I recalled being hungry before we showered. However, once Aaron got his hands on me, I didn't care about food or anything other than what he was doing to my body.

"Now, Megan. I need to be back inside you, now," he demanded.

I raised my lower body but kept my lips on his before reaching my hand between us to guide the tip of his plump dick head to my slick opening. I slid down, spreading myself to accommodate his impressive length and magnificent girth.

Every time I was sure his dick wouldn't all go, but I greedily forced it inside, needing him as deep as my body would allow.

A deep sigh flew past my lips and breezed through locks of his hair, still wet. I slid up and down his glorious dick but knew I wouldn't enjoy the ride for long. He'd revealed in the heat of one of our episodes that I could make him cum in a minute flat if he let me ride him like I was doing right now.

Just as I was thinking it and only after a few long strides, he gripped my ass with gritted teeth.

"You're killing me, Megan, I can't take it. Jesus."

With my ass palmed in his hands, he assisted in controlling my movement, which I didn't mind. His penetrating upward thrust had my eyes rolling in my head.

He knew what my body needed better than I did and managed to send wave after lustful wave of intoxicating levels of pleasure up my pussy that fanned out and spread all over my body.

He had me teetering on the edge of going mad. Pleasure seeped down to my bones, which were threatening to push through my skin and slide clean out of me. I couldn't breathe or think. He fucked every reasonable sense clean out of my head. I couldn't even kiss him right.

My head dropped, and my teeth sank into the taut flesh of his warm shoulder. Over the course of our affair, I decorated him in bite marks, scratches, and even bruises where I'd sucked his skin too hard. He didn't mind, and I couldn't control myself when he made me go out of my head with overwhelming pleasure.

He moaned loudly in my ear, and I didn't know if it was because of my bite or his own pleasure. His heavy breathing joined the sparks of desire that peppered my hot, trembling flesh.

My tits bobbed up and down and rubbed against the soft hairs that dusted his chest. He stretched my walls to the max, making me take him in balls deep. The start of my demise flashed like lightning in my belly before it rose and fell and filled me up from the bottom of my feet to the tips of my hair follicles.

My fingers flexed, tangled in Aaron's hair, gripping a patch at the back of his skull. My nails raked across his scalp before I fisted another handful.

"Aaron! Aaron!" I couldn't stop repeating his name. His magic dick had my brain stuck on his name until I came undone and embraced the sweet, delicious end. The glory took me and dragged me all the way under and out and over.

By the time my mind reattached itself to my brain, Aaron's face was buried in my neck. "God. You feel so fucking good." His dick jerked inside me as he unloaded his hot fluid and shuddered against me, his mind as gone as mine.

Once we overcame our temporary state of orgasmic insanity, our breathing beat out against the nagging groan of the air-conditioning unit and the stale air inside the room was beaten down by our heated sexual aroma.

My heart hammered and when Aaron squeezed me tightly against his chest, I noticed his heart thudding as hard as mine. Just when I believed our connection had gone as deep as it would go, it went further.

He lifted his face and stared into my eyes, and I was helpless to drop my gaze away from his. I was trapped in the emotion the look emitted. The incessant pounding that threatened to blow up my heart shook me with a series piercing shockwaves.

This was a different level of need that charged through me and coated every part of me down to the cellular level. Every inch of my body ached to kiss him, to explore this connection further, but I was afraid. This was that charming monster that had possessed me the day before I left Aaron the first time. Leaving him had proven to be one of the most difficult decisions I'd ever had to make.

I tackled this emotional monster again after Aaron tracked me down. I struggled with it the day he found a way to coax me out of my muted mental state and told me he loved me. I assumed he'd said those words to pull me back from the darkness I had descended into, but it was only now that I knew he meant what he said.

We never expressed what we were to each other. We never defined our relationship. I never said those sacred words back to Aaron, but I couldn't deny what was staring me in the face. I couldn't deny what was coursing through every cell of my body. The way his eyes roved over me now. The softness that lingered in his gaze. The tender kisses that were blossoming between us. Even his touch had softened, mostly only at the beginning and end of our episodes, but it was still something that hadn't been there before.

The unmistakable brushes of intimacy that were knotting us closer together with each passing moment baffled me. We were building a bond so strong that I didn't know if I could walk away from him again when I knew I didn't have any other choice.

We weren't just in lust anymore. We weren't just fucking anymore. We were in something that I didn't want to face. We were face to face with a beast that had the power to destroy not only us but the world in which we knew it. Something that could open our twisted hearts and make us weak when strength was the only way to secure our survival. Something I believed would make Aaron take on whoever was coming after me, no matter how dangerous, how deadly, or how many.

I couldn't let him get killed because of me. I couldn't let him sacrifice whatever time he had left on this planet for me. My brain shut down after I believed he killed my friends, Laura and Beverly. I couldn't imagine what would happen to me if he were killed because of me.

I knew the storm that brewed, and it was meant for me and me alone. I didn't know how I did it. I had no idea how I managed to muddle through the currents that had tugged me so deeply under, but I dropped my gaze away from his and slid from Aaron's lap.

I had never been so afraid of anything in my life as I was of Aaron when this powerful unseen force between us gripped me. I'd rather face the men hunting me. I'd rather face that creature that crawled on my leg in the dark woods. I was less afraid of standing in front of a moving train, than facing Aaron when those powerful uncontrolled emotions showed up and made me feel things that weren't supposed to exist within me for a man I was not supposed to have.

After jumping off his lap like it had been set ablaze, I crawled to the edge of the bed and cradled my shivering body into a tight ball until Aaron's warmth wrapped around me.

"Come here. You're freezing."

I scooted back into his warm embrace, but I couldn't face him, not right now. He pulled the covers over us before resting his face in the crook of my neck. The tender peck he placed on my neck kept the beast nipping at my heart.

"Good night," he said, too sweet to fit his personality.

"Good night," I whispered, still shivering and not because I was cold.

Chapter Twenty-nine

Megan

Aaron was out. His steady breaths flowed against my neck and kept a few loose strands of my hair flapping against my cheek. I couldn't find sleep as easily as he could, not even after two rounds of the most mind-blowing sex between us yet.

His sex usually knocked me out, but not this night. We killed seven people today, and I had stitched up Aaron's side from a knife wound. The vivid memories of violence weren't what kept sleep at bay. I could handle death. What I couldn't handle was what was brewing between Aaron and me.

I laid there, wide awake because I was consumed with my feelings for him. However, the ravaging images of my past would rear its ugly head and rip away any shred of happiness I allowed myself to feel.

Also, that heart-stealing emotion-inducing beast that lingered between me and Aaron had a death grip on me and refused to let go. My twisted heart beat to a new rhythm, one that was an imprint of my connection to his. Aaron didn't call attention to it, but I knew that he felt it too.

This new monster demanded respect. It demanded that I glance deeper than the surface. It demanded your whole heart and delved into your deepest fears and greatest happiness. If you refused any of its demands, it dug in deeper, snatching the little bit of control I possessed. The knowledge that something like this could exist between Aaron and me was the reason I had no other choice but to get away from him.

I turned, only slightly disrupting the hold Aaron had around my waist. He must have been worn out because he didn't move an inch when I turned to face him. He wasn't a snorer, but he breathed heavily, his chest rising and falling rhythmically with each breath.

He had no idea how often I stalked him while he slept. A smile always came to my face when I observed him unconscious and in another world. I wanted to know what he dreamed about. Peace always settled over his sleeping form, no doubt an escape from the not-so-peaceful life he lived.

We'd been too distracted with each other to turn off the lamp, so a dim glow lit my view of Aaron's peaceful face. I ran my hand along his beautifully tattooed body, his tight abs, and muscular arms. I placed a delicate hand over the stitches that marred the smooth skin of his side before leaning up to kiss his warm, soft lips.

"I love you," I whispered against the edge of his lips. Panic hit me when I noticed his top lip twitch and turn up into a small smile. At first, I believed he was awake since he smiled right after I whispered those secret words, but sleep kept him under.

I rolled out of his arms cautiously, but the noisy bed creaked no matter how carefully I maneuvered. A few of the springs poked at me as well and added to the noise of my not-so-hasty getaway.

I glanced back at Aaron several times to make sure I hadn't awakened him. When I was fully standing, I remained in place, staring at him, taking in his handsome face, his chiseled body, and his kissable lips. The bedding covered one of the most masterful parts of him—that glorious dick.

When my staring verged along the lines of being creepy, I headed toward the bathroom. Considering what Aaron and I went through in such a short time, I reckoned creepy wouldn't scare either one of us off.

***

Leaving Florida wasn't a choice for me. It was a necessity. Aaron had tracked me down and caught me because I hadn't moved fast enough. He dragged me back into his life, and it was the last place I needed to be. He'd found me, so could others.

Two weeks had passed since Aaron tracked me down and dragged me back into his intoxicating world. Time with Aaron made it difficult for me to build up the courage I needed to walk away from him again.

Aaron knew about my past. Therefore, he understood me in a way that no one else did. This knowledge also put his life in grave danger.

I loved Aaron, and based on the tears that wouldn't stop flowing down my warm cheeks, I loved him a lot more than I'd been willing to admit to myself.

I didn't know how he'd done it. I didn't know how he'd been able to unfreeze my twisted heart and make me love him so much. However, my love for Aaron was the reason I had to leave him, and I didn't think he would understand it if I tried to explain. I took one last glimpse at his handsome sleeping face before I turned the lock on the wobbly doorknob and inched the door closed behind me.

I stood against the outside of our cheap motel room, wiping my tears, praying that I was doing the right thing. I was a walking, talking, living, breathing target. Of course, I was doing the right thing.

Anyone near or around me would end up murdered and it was why I stayed away from Beverly and Laura. Was there a chance that the assassins we encountered could have been after Aaron's MC and not me? Yes, but my instincts were telling me that they were after me.

So, here I was, Lacey Daniels, a.k.a. Megan Jones, running away from Aaron for the second time. I managed to leave him sleeping on the other side of the door that my trembling body leaned against. The things he was willing to do to protect me made the grip on my heart squeeze harder.

Him carrying around equipment and weapons that contended with the weapons of hired assassins was positive proof that he could protect me in a battle, but I refused to let him go to war over me.

My face bunched into a tight knot as I fought to hold in my sobs. The ugly-cry had taken over and turned me into a blundering mess as I moved over the dark road with my mouth wide-opened and allowed my cries to float into the darkness. I didn't want to leave him, but what else was I supposed to do?

After stumbling around the dark wood-lined street for hours attempting to figure out my next move, I believed I finally had a plan.

It didn't take long for my smile to dissipate as my mind fell right back on Aaron. By now, he'd have woken up and discovered that I'd run away from him, again. He was going to hate me for it, especially after him admitting that he loved me. He also admitted that he was willing to fight for me no matter if the assassins were after his MC or me. He didn't say it outright, but his actions spoke much louder than his words.

This wasn't Aaron's fight, and I wasn't going to sit by and let him fight my battle. In all my lessons in survival, running was my best option, so I ran. I was the one who sought out dangerous situations, therefore I should be the one to suffer the consequences of my actions.

I was so distracted about leaving Aaron that I somehow managed to ignore the call of animals lurking in the woods as I wandered through the darkness. The prancing feet of four-legged creatures likely large enough to rip me to pieces roamed nearby as I ambled over the dark asphalt covered highway surrounded by woods. The lights of the cheap motel about a quarter mile ahead of me had never looked so sweet.

A bell chimed over the door alerting the front desk clerk of my approach. A portly middle-aged woman didn't bother speaking but flashed me a fake smile.

"Double's all we got. That okay?"

The clerk leveled an irritated look at me for taking too long to respond.

"Yes, a double will be fine," I answered.

"Thank you," I called back to the clerk as I dashed away with quick, choppy steps. I hoped like hell that leaving Aaron meant that I was leading the bad guys away from him.

Chapter Thirty

Aaron

I jumped up with a start. My breaths heaved as my chest bobbed up and down with quick jerky movements. The scene in the woods with the mercenaries had gone down differently in my dream.

In the dream, they captured Megan and held a gun to her head. Her big, terrified eyes begged me for help, but I was powerless to do anything but stand there and watch. Just as the blast from the gun sounded, I lurched from the mattress.

A cool layer of sweat coated my body as my sore muscles twitched beneath my damp skin. Shaking off the nightmare, I reached out for Megan, but she wasn't lying next to me. The spot was cool. She'd been up for a while. My gaze traveled to the closed bathroom door, listening for her.

Megan believed the men who attacked us were meant for her. She stressed that her past would get me killed. What she didn't know was that I didn't care if those men had come for her because I had a problem with anyone who threatened to bring harm to her.

I would go to war for any member of my club, no matter how misguided they were, and no matter if we were feuding internally. And I realized while the bullets were flying that I was willing to die to save Megan too. I was willing to bring death to anyone who threatened to harm a hair on her head.

She wanted to leave me, and although she wouldn't admit it, I knew that if she left me this time, not only was she not coming back to me, but she would make it so I never find her again.

The idea of not seeing Megan was an unbearable first for me. Shit between us had gone past me craving the best sex of my life. It had moved to care, understanding, and that unseen force that could send the manliest man to his knees.

If I lost Megan, I would lose my fucking mind. She grounded me, made me believe my life was worth a damn. That I was not just passing along in a blur of boring days until someone needed the next body to drop or the guns to get collected and distributed. If protecting Megan was my purpose, I would gladly accept the job.

My eyes darted to the bathroom door again. It was awfully quiet in there. I lugged my stiff body from the squeaky bed and padded to the bathroom. I twisted the knob, sprang the door open, and peered in. No Megan.

The crease in my forehead deepened as I instinctively checked every crack and corner of the shabby motel room, knowing that Megan wasn't inside. Wishful thinking made me ignore the obvious.

I glanced at the bags of groceries we'd gotten before the shootout, sitting in a neat pile near the loud air-conditioning unit. *Maybe she went to the vending machine.*

My speeding heart and quickened pulse had me pacing around the room like I was missing a part of my soul and didn't know what to do without that missing part. There was no way anyone had taken her right from under my nose. I'm sure they would be dead on the floor if they had tried.

After throwing on my clothes, I snatched the room key from the wobbly cigarette-burned table and dashed out of the door.

I searched for Megan on the first level where we were and the second level near the vending machines. My heart picked up its pace, and my internal senses screamed that she'd taken off.

"I can't let anything happen to you because of me." Those were the words she'd said to me after the shootout in the woods.

My fingers skimmed the back pocket of my jeans before I withdrew my wallet. It had just occurred to me that it was in my left pocket, and I always tucked it into my right. I flipped it open and found nothing but lint inside. Megan had taken the few hundred in cash I carried and in its place, was a neatly folded note on the hotel's cheap stationery.

I unfolded the note, my gaze locked on to her scribbled words.

Aaron. I know that those men were after me, and I can't let them hurt you any worse than they already have because of my actions. You are the best thing that's ever happened in my life, and I'll always cherish and remember our time together, but I must pay for my own sins.

Megan.

What the fuck kind of wimpy goodbye was that? What was up with her and goodbyes? Why didn't she tell me to my face that she was ready to leave? *Because you would have talked her out of it like you've been doing for the past week.*

My fucking hand began to shake as a tornado tunneled its way through my brain. Finding Megan was my number one priority. She was out there running around alone with a group of armed mercenaries on the loose.

If there was one thing I'd come to realize, it was that Megan was a part of me. A part that I'd rip this fucking world apart to protect. But first, I needed to find her— *again.*

Megan was insistent that the group hunting us was after her, and was therefore sure she believed she was doing the right thing by leaving me. It no longer mattered who the group was hunting, both our pasts were dark enough that madness and mayhem was a part of us.

Even if this group of mercenaries were looking for her, it didn't mean that I would stand by and let someone harm her.

I drove by and checked out the other two motels on the stretch of back-woods roads we decided to lodge on. I would have called D, to track Megan's phone, but the woman had kept so much from me, that I didn't even know her phone number.

After driving around for two frantic hours searching for her, an idea seeped its way into my brain and made me ease my foot down on the accelerator.

Megan was a clever woman, but she gave me a glimpse into the way she contemplated certain situations.

The first time I was hunting for her, I traveled across multiple states and had to use illegally acquired information to find out that she was right under my nose, here in Florida. If it hadn't been for D, I probably wouldn't have found her.

Would she do it again? Would Megan hide right under my nose as I chased her ghost? There was only one way to find out, and I prayed my hunch was right.

Chapter Thirty-one

Aaron

I knocked on the hotel door and waited for the occupant to answer. The line of light above the thick burnt-orange curtains in the wide dusty window let me know that someone was inside.

My hard knock made the door vibrate as the sound of insects congregating in the nearby woods buzzed in my ears.

"Front desk," I called out before my knuckles struck the door again.

I stepped away from the view of the peephole, hoping that the front desk attendant I questioned wasn't one of those people who saw a person and forgot what they looked like five minutes later. I described Megan to the woman down to the part on the right side of her head that split her lengthy thick dark curls.

The shadow that passed across the peephole alerted me that someone was at the door although I hadn't heard any footsteps.

The *click* of the lock turning made my heartrate kick up a notch. Needing to know, eagerly waiting, I prayed it was Megan. When the door creaked open, the chain stopped it from going too far, but there was no mistaking those big beautiful brown eyes that searched through the crack, those lush, soft lips, and the soft tone of her voice.

"Can I help you?"

She jumped and staggered back and away from the crack in the door with her hand over her heart when I placed my face directly in front of hers.

"Open the door, Megan!" I was both angry and relieved.

She stood staring through the crack at me, mouth agape, hand shaking as it covered her heart.

I closed my eyes and sighed when she closed the door, and the chain sliding on the other side sounded. She stepped back, stood behind the door, and cracked it open. I didn't storm inside, although every cell in my body wanted to get her into my arms as quickly as possible.

The sight of her and the knowledge that I almost lost her had me jittery. A raw, edgy sensation had me breathing hard, almost gasping to get air into my lungs.

As soon as she closed and locked the door, I tugged her into my arms so fast she released a muffled *humph*. I couldn't control my shaking body as I encircled her in my arms. I squeezed her way too tight, but I was admittedly helpless when it came to this woman.

"I thought I lost you. Don't do that shit to me again. I can't fucking lose you, Megan." I buried my face in her neck, savoring her sweet scent and the comfort of having her in my arms. I was beginning to think that she was my purpose for being alive. What other reason could I have for feeling this way about someone?

Her soft fluffy curls brushed over my stubbly face and neck, and I relished the soft texture sweeping over my skin. I craved the sparks Megan brought to my life, the tingles she sent racing up and down my spine, and even the all-consuming confusion and helpless state she had the ability to throw me into.

When I managed to release her from my tight grip, a stream of tears rolled down her cheeks. Hands that were way too delicate to be mine, cupped either side of her face, swiping away tears as I tilted her face up to meet mine.

"Megan. I don't give a good goddamn who's after you or why. I'm not going to let anything happen to you."

"But..."

"There are no buts," I stated firmly and with finality.

Her gaze searched mine. My gaze pinned hers, attempting to get her to understand that I was not going to abandon her, no matter what.

"Promise me that you're not going to leave me again, Megan. Please."

It must have been the 'please,' a word I was not known for using often, if ever, that got her attention.

She shook her head as her tears began to fall quicker. I kept her face clinched in my palms until she said, out loud, what I wanted to hear.

"I won't leave you again," she forced out through her cracked voice. "I promise."

At those words, she went crashing back into my chest from me drawing her in once more. How I'd gotten by without this woman in my life was a mystery that would likely take me a lifetime to figure out.

I couldn't stop hugging her, my joy at finding her overwhelmed me, and I was unable to get the build-up of emotions out of my system. I eased out of the hug, letting my lips brush her cheek before I captured her lips, tasting her salty tears.

It only took a moment for the sparks to ignite between us and for my tongue to go searching for hers. Only when my body threatened to give out from lack of oxygen, did I stop kissing her and leaned my forehead against hers.

"We don't know what's going to happen with this group hunting us. But, as long as we stick together, Megan, we are going to be okay." I paused. She needed to let my words sink in.

"Do you understand what I'm telling you?"

"Yes. You're not going to let anything happen to me as long as we stick together," spilled out in a low and unsteady tone. Her words didn't sound convincing enough for me.

Our future may have been a little cloudy, dark even, but if we were together, I believed with all my heart and soul that we were going to be alright. Even if Megan didn't have someone from her past chasing her that she'd likely pissed off, there was still the fact that my life was a fucking revolving door of mayhem too. Either way, she wasn't ever going to outrun danger, so she may as well get used to facing it.

Besides, letting her go was not something I was willing to accept right now, if ever.

"Megan, there is nothing, absolutely nothing that I'd admit out loud to being afraid of, except, losing you. Don't you understand that you're all that matters to me now? The only thing that makes sense among all these years of chaos that my life has been."

Her gaze frantically searched mine before she found words.

"You remember what happened to me when you told me that you killed Beverly and Laura?"

A small smile crept across my lips before I placed a tender kiss on hers. "Yes, I remember, and I'm sorry I did that to you."

She shook her head, seemingly forcing out her words.

"If something happened to you because of me, it would be worse than a mental blackout. I wouldn't come back. I wouldn't want to. It would permanently break me. That's why I left Aaron. I'd rather leave knowing you're okay, than face...than face..."

My death.

She couldn't even say the words.

Her fingers tightened around my arms driving her words deeper. "It would be worse than what Carlos did to me."

She literally ripped my heart out with those words. No one had ever cared that much about me. I swallowed the fucking lump of emotions choking and preventing me from talking. I paused, breathing through the river of feelings swirling inside me. What did I ever do to deserve this level of affection?

I understood what Megan was saying better than she assumed I did. This deep connection we shared, it baffled me, but I couldn't help embracing it even though it scared the shit out of me.

"I can't do it, Megan," I said, shaking my head.

"Can't do what?" she questioned. Her forehead creased as she stared into my eyes. I was sure I resembled a fucked up mad man to her. I sure as shit felt like one.

"I can't let you go. If something happened to you, and I hadn't done everything in my power to help you or save you, I wouldn't just break, Megan. I would break the fucking world until there was nothing left of it or me."

Her mouth parted and closed a few times, but she was too stunned to say anything. I tilted her head up, making sure she saw clearly into my eyes and understood the meaning of every word I was about to say. I was about to be the corniest motherfucker on the planet, but I didn't care. Megan deserved to know how I felt.

"Megan. I love you. I'm fucking insanely in love with you, and I don't give a damn if there's a fucking army after you. I promise that I'll protect you as long as there is life inside my body."

My words had left her frozen and staring at me, lips moving without words. She blinked away the tears that pooled in her eyes before placing her palms against my chin.

"I love you too," she murmured as her anxious fingers left my face and dug into my neck and shoulders. "So much, it scares me."

No other words were necessary. She went up on her toes and sent her lips crashing into mine this time. And we didn't stop fondling each other until we were butt-ass naked in room 129. Three doors down from 123, in the same cheap ass motel Megan left me in hours ago.

End of Twisted Hearts

Excerpt

Twisted Secrets Book #3

Synopsis

Megan: How the hell did he do it? Aaron messed with my mind and twisted up my heart, but my body had never been so splendidly ravaged. Stepping away from the August Knights Motorcycle Club was easy, but leaving Aaron was killing me. Was it crazy of me to want to subject myself to the madness the group stood for because I couldn't shake Aaron's hold on me? I couldn't go back. I had to consider his safety. I couldn't allow my twisted past to go crashing into the turbulent life he led.

Aaron: How the hell did she do it? Megan had cracked my chest open and filled it with a riot of crippling emotions I couldn't shake. Letting Megan go wasn't easy. Was it crazy of me to go chasing her after we agreed that it was over? I had to find her. My infatuation with her didn't leave me any other options. In my quest to find Megan, I discovered that she had secrets, deep dark ones I could have figured out if I hadn't gotten distracted. I would make her tell me what she was hiding in that twisted mind of hers—*or else.*

Part I

Chapter One

Aaron

It's been two weeks since I tracked Megan down and brought her back to my house. I was supposed to find her and kill her for infiltrating my MC, but my dick stopped me. For as strong-willed as I believed I was, for once in my life, my dick was right.

Not killing Megan had led me to finding out how she ended up the way she had mentally. The story behind her actions was so gut-wrenching that it justified her twisted behavior.

Yesterday, we killed seven men together after they chased and followed us into a patch of Copper County's thick woods. We left. They didn't.

Once we fled the scene and settled, Megan ran from me again. I don't believe I would have another problem with her running from me anymore. As her punishment, I gave her a fucking she won't soon forget. I had her ass praying on her hands and knees for me to stop.

In all honesty, I didn't know it was possible for someone like me, with a heart as black as coal, to love someone so deeply. I would do anything for Megan—rob, cheat, commit murder—anything. She likely assumed I was talking out of my ass when I told her as much, but I meant every word. If someone harmed a hair on her head, they would know my wrath.

I glanced at her in the dim light of the early morning, lying against the passenger's door panel of my truck. She'd passed out on the drive back to my house since I'd kept her up all night.

As I drove, I recalled the men who were hunting us. There was no way of confirming who the mercenaries were hunting yesterday—her or me. Logic stated they were a group after Megan because my usual suspects were bikers, gang members, or the occasional wanna-be gangsters making a name for themselves.

The guys I led into the woods yesterday had come out of nowhere and struck with military precision. They had opened fire in a busy grocery store parking lot. It meant they didn't care about killing innocent victims if it meant taking out their target.

My MC was comprised of hundreds of members spread over five states, and we had many enemies. Megan was only one woman. Who the hell was after her that could not only afford hired guns but who could also afford to track her? If I hadn't known about her books and D hadn't followed the money trail to her friends, I would probably still be searching for her.

The Russians had come at our MC years ago with the same level of aggression as the assassins that attacked us yesterday. It's one of the reasons I kept military-grade weaponry in my possession.

The men yesterday spoke Spanish, of that, I was sure. I couldn't recall our MC having a beef with any Hispanic groups, but I had to consider that there were a few of us known for stirring up trouble; the kind of trouble that led to dead bodies.

A flicker of light flashing across my cracked driver's side mirror drew my attention. I glanced at Megan who was still out before I leaned up and squinted to get a better view of the squad car behind us. Most of the Copper County cops left my MC alone as long as we kept our drama out of the public's eyes and laced their pockets.

"Shit," I mumbled as I took in the shadows of two cops inside the car. My truck looked like it had taken a slow stroll through hell, and two unfamiliar Copper County Police officers were pulling me over. When they saw Megan, they were going to take whatever they had planned to the next level.

To make matters worse, we were on a stretch of back-woods roads surrounded by trees, so these asshole cops could do whatever the hell they wanted and get away with it.

Maintaining careful movements, I reached over and took the gun Megan had wedged between her hip and the console and placed it under my seat. I did the same to the one I had tucked in my waist.

"Megan," I called out after I shook her shoulder. She jumped up, frantically searching her surroundings, thinking we were under attack. In a way, we were about to get attacked if the mean scowls on the officers' faces as they exited the black and white squad car was any indication.

I hadn't spotted them on the highway, so they had likely been parked off the roadway, painting their lips with powdered sugar when they spotted me.

My eyes remained on the officers in the mirror as I talked to Megan.

"We are being pulled over by the cops. I don't know these assholes, so I'm going to need you to stay quiet and answer only what they ask you."

"Okay," she said, stretching her neck to look back. She reached for the gun I'd already hidden.

"I put it under my seat. Stay still," I told her, my voice projecting my agitation although nothing had happened yet.

The officers approached my truck from both sides, taking careful sideways steps. The sight of my damaged vehicle riddled with bullet holes caused them to grip their pistols as they drew and aimed them at the ground.

They stopped at the back edge of the sides of my truck. One had his eyes on me in my mirror, the other I presumed kept an eye on Megan's door as her side mirror had been shot off the truck.

When they stepped out and away from the tail end of my truck and turned toward me and Megan with their weapons aimed at our heads, I closed my eyes and prayed. I prayed that I wasn't going to have to take the life of two Copper County police officers.

"Roll the windows all the way down and both of you stick your hands through the opening!" The one on my side shouted the words as he edged closer to my position. My gaze was locked on him in the mirror.

"Any sudden movements and we will kill you. I'll blow your fucking head off your shoulders!" he shouted. My irritation was heightened by the cocky arrogance in his voice.

As I cautiously reached my hands through my window, I glanced at Megan doing the same. We just couldn't catch a break. Was three or four days without drama too much to ask for?

The closer the officer came to me, the more I was convinced that this situation was only going to get uglier. The unmistakable sound of his approaching steps drew him close enough to reveal his cracked reflection in the mirror.

I focused on a fixed location in the mirror that allowed me to see the deep frown on his face. The steady aim of his gun at my head kept me quiet, but nothing would take away my hostile nature, my own mean grimace, or the liquid fire coursing through my veins.

"I'm going to open this door and you're going to be a good dog and move out of that seat slowly."

An angry growl escaped when he called me a dog. Now, able to see him standing outside my door, he took the gun in one hand and kept it aimed at my head as he used his other hand to open my door.

Just as my door started to creak open, the other officer yelled, "What the fuck? Joe, do you see this shit. Look who he has in the truck with him."

Upon hearing his friend's discovery of Megan, Joe's fucking finger flexed on the trigger and damn near sent my brains all over the back of my seat.

Joe edged his gun closer to my head as he leaned forward and peeked around me. His eyes remained on Megan a long time before they landed back on me. Disgust was written all over his face. Every frown line he had stretched tighter and deepened.

"So, you're one of those confused motherfuckers, huh? You like that black poontang?" he spat his questions at me. "Step out of this truck, son, I'm about to teach you what your fucking father should have taught you when you were younger," he barked his angry words, his voice laced with pure hate.

I rolled my shoulder and eased out of my truck, taking a deep and steadying breath. The partner hadn't asked Megan to get out yet, and I hope he had sense enough to leave her alone.

As soon as the first pebble crunched under my boot, I was snatched by the shoulder and shoved toward the hood of my truck.

"Get out of the truck, n*gg*r girl," the partner said to Megan as my face was being pressed into the dented hood of my truck. The jagged metal nudged angrily at my skin, eager to slice a hole in my face.

Movement on the other side of my truck captured my attention, but I couldn't see anything with my face turned in the opposite direction. My head was trapped between the twisted metal of my hood and the barrel of Officer Joe's gun as he shoved it into my cheek.

"You are going to learn today," he whispered harshly, placing his mouth close to my ear as he leaned into me. His hot breath rained over my face as a few sprinkles of spittle dotted my cheek.

The sound of Megan's whimper caused me to resist as I struggled to get up.

"You better be still before I blow yours and that black bitch's brains all over this highway. I'll leave your asses in those woods as dinner for the maggots and worms."

Patience. Patience. Patience. I repeated inside my head. If I made the wrong move, it could lead to Megan being harmed.

"Can you believe this shit, Cass? I believe this motherfucker is willing to die for that black bitch."

I could hear Megan taking deep breaths and wasn't sure if the officer had her pressed over the hood or not. My body was coiled so tightly that there was no way the asshole standing over me wasn't being poisoned by my anger.

Officer Cass began. His deep voice projected over my hood, "I'd never do some backwards shit like this, but I could certainly understand the appeal, especially with this one."

"Cass, shut your dumb ass up. If your father heard you say some dumb shit like that, he'd punch you in the fucking mouth."

The butt of the officer's service gun sank deeper into my jaw and the tight bitterness in his voice intensified. "What's your name, son? I need to know who I'm about to give lessons to."

I didn't answer because I was consumed with images of the best way of taking these motherfuckers out without getting Megan killed in the process. My fists tightened, sounding like I was cracking walnuts.

"I said, what's your motherfucking name, asshole!" The words oozed slowly between the officer's clenched teeth. His hatred at seeing me with Megan had him about to lose his life because I was at the end of my rope.

The low tone of Megan's voice sounded and snapped me out of the hot zone, but I couldn't understand her words.

"Shut the fuck up, bitch. I didn't tell you to talk!" Officer Cass yelled.

"Look at his cut!" Megan yelled, disobeying a direct order from the racist cop.

Patience had vacated my body entirely and I shook from the effort it took to contain my rage. The treaty we had with the Copper County Police Department was about to be ripped to shreds along with this bastard's body.

"Joe," his partner called in a low tone laced with concern. Joe didn't answer his partner because he was too busy taunting me with his vicious words.

"Joe!" his partner yelled his name this time, his voice dripping with nervous tension.

"What? Don't you see I'm busy over here?"

"Joe, look at his vest."

Joe's grip on my neck eased as did the gun he had pressed damn near through the side of my cheek.

"August Knights," he read out my MC's name in a low tone. Then dead silence fell over the scene for what seemed like an eternity. A slow wind swept through the leaves of the surrounding trees, making it sound like they were applauding the officer's ability to read and determine that he was flirting with death.

Joe's tight grip left my neck and so did the butt of his gun from my cheek. His shoes scraping the concrete sounded as he backed away from me. I eased up, lifting to an upright position.

The first place my eyes went to was Megan standing on the other side of my hood with the officer standing uncomfortably behind her. Brows pinched and eyes begging for mercy, the sorry sack of shit knew he had fucked up.

"Are you okay?" I asked Megan, not giving a damn about the dicks standing behind us.

She nodded, keeping her gaze locked on mine.

"Did he put his fucking hands on you?" I spit my words over the hood at the stone-faced officer standing behind Megan.

"No," she said in a shaky tone as her gaze landed on the officer standing silently behind me. He hadn't said a word since he read the words on my cut. Megan had no idea our MC had a long history with the police in Copper County. How did she know to tell the cop to look at my cut?

"Hey, man, I didn't know you were an August Knight," the one behind Megan shuddered.

"Me either. I just transferred down here four months ago," Joe, the one behind me said in a humble tone.

His partner standing behind Megan had his weapon holstered and had both his hands raised in surrender. "Look, man," he said, shaking his head. "I don't want any trouble with your group. I didn't know who you were until I got a good enough look at your vest."

"Let's go, Megan," I said as I dusted my hands over my clothes. Then, I reared back and socked the motherfucker behind me in the face so hard his nose crunched under my fist.

He fell to the ground, landing on his ass as he clutched his nose, blood oozing between his fingers. He scrambled back when I moved, thinking I would hit him again.

Instead, I moved toward my open truck door. I didn't even glance back at the officer. I was afraid to look at him because of the twisted shit my mind kept yelling for me to do. I needed to be away from this situation because I wasn't sure I had the strength to contain the obscene amount of rage coursing through me.

Once we were back in the truck I sat, gripping the steering wheel. Hunched, the bloody-faced officer walked briskly back to his squad car. His partner had already retreated to the vehicle.

"Are you okay?" Megan asked, her soft tone easing a little of my tension. The haze of rage that surrounded me began to fade away and the world started to sound and return to normal again.

"I'm good," I told her, my angry tone indicating I was anything but good. She reached across and placed a hand on my arm, which shook with tension under her soft touch.

"It's okay. We're okay," she reassured, and I didn't know if she was asking a question or making a statement.

My gaze landed on the hand she had placed on my arm before I glanced over at her. "You and I, we are always going to be okay. I just need a moment."

With that, she dropped her hand and allowed me to take my moment. Mentally, I soothed my nerves as close to calm as I could get them. I started my truck and drove off, leaving those asshole cops sitting in their car. The sight of them grew smaller in my cracked mirror as I proceeded to my destination.

Those police officers had no idea the person they were taught to hate had just saved their lives. Even now, I wanted to turn around and release my rage by pounding on their bodies, but I had more important things to worry about. I had to figure out who was hunting Megan and me and more importantly, how to stop them.

Chapter Two

Aaron

We were just in a situation that could have turned deadly and Megan sat next to me as cool as a cucumber. My tension had eased as well.

"How did you know to tell that cop to look at my cut?"

She smiled before glancing in my direction. "I didn't know if it would work, but after hearing what you and your father were talking about on the phone and after your father started allowing me to enter the board room during meetings, I concluded that you all had ties with law enforcement."

"That was smart," I complimented her, making her smile deepen. I hadn't even considered explaining who I was to the cops. Megan was in danger, so all I saw was red. She was my weakness, and I needed to find a way to balance caring for her and handling my business as usual.

I avoided the normal route to my house, although it was off the beaten path. I took the scenic drive which was an overgrown path through the woods that would take me to within a stone's throw of my house. It was the same path I took when I discovered that Chuck and his crew had landed on my doorstep.

The knowledge that Megan was in my house alone with them had driven me past the point of madness. It was the first time I realized I would do anything to protect her, even if it meant giving myself up.

I'd ditched my truck in the woods that day. After snooping around and discovering the men hadn't harmed Megan, I snuck into the house. If I hadn't feared Megan being shot in a gun battle, I would have handled Chuck, Clint, and Dutch in an entirely different manner.

My actions that day marked the first time I acknowledged my weakness. My being careful had nearly gotten both of us killed. Megan saved my life that day. Although my intent was to avoid a gun battle, she'd initiated one that had lured us away from the grips of death.

The idea that a group like Chuck's had lurked long enough to find my house made me aware that this new group may have the means to find a way to my doorstep as well. How long had this group been in town? How long had they been watching Megan, me and my MC?

Last night, I warned my MC about the dangerous group lingering, but I wasn't worried. For as dumb as they sometimes acted, when it came to life or death, they would choose life and survival by any means necessary.

I found a spot, plush with thick trees and vines to park in the woods behind my house. I made a move to climb out of my truck, but Megan stopped me, gripping my arm.

"I want to come," she insisted.

I said the magic word, "Please," and she stayed put in the truck. She was afraid to let me out of her sight now that I had confirmed my loyalty to her.

My boot-clad feet trounced across the roots of trees and broken twigs as I crept closer to my house. Instincts told me that after that shootout yesterday, this group already knew who we were. If they were after Megan, they may have tracked her to my MC.

When the back of my house came into view, everything appeared normal, but I approached with caution.

I opened the back door using the key I left tucked in a secret nook above the door frame. A flick of the knob sent the door creaking open. A tap of the metal tip of my gun sent the door swinging over the area where Clint's dead body had lain a month prior.

My gun remained aimed and ready to fire as the cold steel of my back-up pistol rested against my lower back. Although the house was in order, careful steps led me through my kitchen as I kept my ears peeled for lurkers.

When I stepped into my bedroom, my gaze landed on the area where my safe room was hidden. The thick boxed headboard of my bed kept the entrance of the space hidden. A smaller room sat snugly between the walk-in closet and bathroom. I was the only one who knew about the secret space since I reduced the size of my closet to build it.

Attached to the wall of the hidden room, I strategically constructed my headboard which contained a latch to release it from the wall. The half door hidden behind my headboard opened into the closet-size safe-room.

After reaching into the thick wooden front of the headboard, I unlatched it from the wall. Two forceful heaves sent the bed out of my way. I kneeled before the half door and entered the combination that sprung the door open.

Within minutes, I entered the room, retrieved money, extra guns, ammunition, and re-concealed the location. I packed myself a bag, packed Megan's backpack with the items of hers that I could find and headed out in case there was a lookout watching the house.

Megan and I needed to regroup so we could plan our next move. We needed to figure out who the hell was hunting us. Even if they weren't initially hunting me, my actions in those woods put my MC and me on their radar. However, when they attempted to take my life and Megan's, they had inadvertently placed themselves on my radar as well.

I walked away from the house that I'd lived in for three years not knowing when I would return. The last few drops of dew glistened off leaves as the sun rose higher in the sky. The hike back to my truck went by in a blur.

My mind worked overtime, processing the group of mercenaries we encountered yesterday. I was hesitant to say the word mercenaries in front of Megan, not that she couldn't handle it, but she had been through enough. I didn't want her to stress or worse, have her take off on me again.

Of all the things she should have been worried about, she was worried about me being in harm's way. *Me.* When my own mother was alive, she didn't care that much about me. Knowing that someone cared if I lived or died put a spark of color in my heart and brought a smile to my face.

Chapter Three

Aaron

My internal sensor for picking up threats had my eyes jetting around the area that led to our MC's clubhouse. I'd lived surrounded by danger for so long that I sensed it. The dead, empty air swept into my rolled-down windows and filled the cab space of my truck. The air alone told a story I was not ready to hear yet.

The bullet holes in the wood siding of the clubhouse were visible through my dusty windshield as I drove closer. The busted front window and the front door hanging lopsided told me all I needed to know.

I turned onto a trail and drove my truck farther into the woods to keep it hidden. Once I found a good enough spot, I glanced at Megan.

"Stay in the truck and put one of those guns in your hands."

No questions, no back talk, only actions. This was one of the reasons why I loved Megan. She reached down next to her sexy-ass hip and made the Beretta appear. The familiar slide and clap of the weapon being charged made my mouth inch into a smile, despite what I might face inside our clubhouse.

I scanned my surroundings once more while I exited my truck with my weapon aimed and ready to put a hole in someone. At 08:45 a.m., it was too early for anyone but my father to be at the clubhouse.

The front end of his truck peeked from the far side of the house where I knew it would be parked. My father slept at the clubhouse more than he stayed in his house. I reckon he preferred the clubhouse more because it had been his and my mother's home. He claimed they were happy there once. How anyone, even my father, could have been happy with my hateful mother was beyond me.

There were no visible dead bodies in the area. There was no spilled blood. But, the broken glass on the ground indicated that my father had at least shot back at someone. Therefore, he was either dead, dying, or inside killing someone. Entertaining the idea of my father being dead sent rage blazing through my veins.

As much as my father got on my nerves, I loved the old crow. However, there was one thing I knew well about him. He was a fighter. He would go up against the Devil if it came to it.

The faint scent of vehicle exhaust lingered in the air mixed with the unmistakable scent of freshly fired guns. Whoever had been here, hadn't been gone long and could double back. Several bullet casings dotted the ground, and the deep imprint left by tires scratching on the graveled parking area in front of the clubhouse was visible.

I glanced back to make sure no one was creeping up behind me. The toe of my boot is what I used to ease the lopsided screen door further open. Shards of glass fell from the square panes that once framed the heavy door, alerting anyone inside to my entrance. Once the door was open, I swept around and let the barrel of my pistol lead the way.

"Dad!" I called out. "You alive?"

Out stumbled my father with a gun jammed down the front of his pants. He had another gun aimed, and it was leading him out of the double doors of the kitchen.

"Motherfucking bastards shot me in the shoulder. I called Karla to come and pluck this bullet out and sew me up," he muttered, spewing a slew of curse words.

Karla was a nurse my father had dated off and on for years. Although she was married and about twenty years his junior, whenever he called her to patch up an injured member of our MC, she came without question.

He stepped into plain view. His faded black T-shirt was wet with blood as it clung to his shoulder and chest area. I should have been more worried, considering how bloody he was, but he was a tough old bird that didn't like to be coddled.

"Fucking mercenaries, like you said. I think they came here as a warning. If they wanted me dead, you would be standing over my empty meatsuit right now. They were in a black SUV with tinted windows. When one stepped out of the vehicle, and I saw a gun in his hand with a silencer attached, I didn't wait around to see what the fuck they wanted. I started shooting, and they sure as shit didn't mind shooting back."

The people we were dealing with weren't bikers, and I seriously doubted they were an enemy of the MC. Megan may have been right that these assholes were after her.

"Who the fuck are these people, Aaron?" my father asked. He knew I should've had an answer to that question by now. I was willing to go to war over Megan but it damn sure didn't mean my father or the rest of my MC were willing.

"I don't know who the fuck they are," I replied. "We deal in guns and drugs, so it could be a faction aiming to take over our gun business."

My father shook his head, his mind obviously running wild about who was targeting us. My flimsy excuse would work on the rest of the club, but my father knew better.

I didn't like the quiet amusement in his eyes as he stared me down.

"I called your cousin, Ansel," he revealed as a wicked smirk creased his face. His revelation left me speechless for a few moments.

"Why the fuck did you do that? Why the fuck didn't you at least wait until I figured out who the hell these people are?" I rolled my eyes at my father before pinching the bridge of my nose.

"Dad, you know as well as I do, Cousin Ansel's ass is as crazy as fuck and he's as out of control as these damn mercenaries. He likes to kill for the fun of it and he and his band of killers don't give two fucks about who dies as long as somebody goes to hell."

I attempted but failed to shake off the ideas of my crazy-ass cousin. Two years ago, I left the MC for two months to help our gun supplier with a little problem they had that could've demolished our gun deal entirely. While I was away, my father ran into a little trouble with a rival

MC. Long story short, the MC became extinct after my father called my cousin, Ansel, for his brand of help.

Ansel and his crew ate through a third of the motorcycle club and killed over twenty-five men in less than a week. The rest of the MC scattered or had gone into hiding for all we knew. We never heard anything else from them after Ansel got a hold of them. The Feds and every agency in the country was still sniffing around for some of the bodies.

Cousin Ansel was who you called whenever you'd run out of options, not when you hadn't even figured out the problem yet. I cupped my forehead and rubbed my tired eyes. "How long before he arrives?" I asked my father.

Ansel lived and worked illegally out of California. He was a member of our MC and often joined us whenever we gathered and went on group bike rides.

"He said he'd be here sometime tomorrow," my father answered with that smirk still on his face.

I leveled him with a hard stare and prayed that his injured shoulder was hurting like hell. He threw up his palm on his good side in reaction to my angry glare.

"What did you expect me to do? You called me last night telling me you and that black wife of yours had dropped seven bodies in the woods. Next thing I know, the damn television was lit up with dead bodies and a blown-up car like a fucking war had taken place in those woods. Before the day hardly breaks, motherfuckers are blowing holes in the clubhouse with silenced weapons."

When he put it that way, it did sound bad. I was too busy searching for and fucking Megan, my, *black wife*, as my father had so elegantly put it, to care about checking out the news.

He leaned in and lowered his voice like someone was listening to us. "Is *she* with you now?" Him referring to Megan as my wife meant he'd managed to swallow his pride and accept that I was not going to get rid of her.

"Yeah. You got a problem with it?" I asked, daring him with my gaze to say something stupid.

He shook his long, crooked finger at me. "You know fucking well I got a problem with it, but we got bigger problems to worry about than you claiming a woman who's forbidden to us."

He shook his head, his loud laughter irking my fucking nerves. The damn smirk had returned to his smug face.

"You know how Ansel is. What do you think he's going to do when he sees your new woman?"

The ache in my head grew sharper, and my left eye started to twitch. The idea of what Ansel might do once he found me with Megan sent my blood pressure shooting through the roof.

"Dad, stop flapping your damn gums and make yourself useful. Warn everybody about what's going on so they can be ready if more shit goes down. To be on the safe side, send them to the safe houses. I'm going to do some sniffing around. If they found the clubhouse, someone who knows us was likely bought and has sold us out or was tortured and forced to talk. But that doesn't matter. The motherfuckers came at us, so either—"

"They die or we die," my father and I said the statement simultaneously. Whenever we went into survival mode, that specific statement was tossed around a lot. Crazy thing was, we meant it.